The Hero
Two Doors
Down

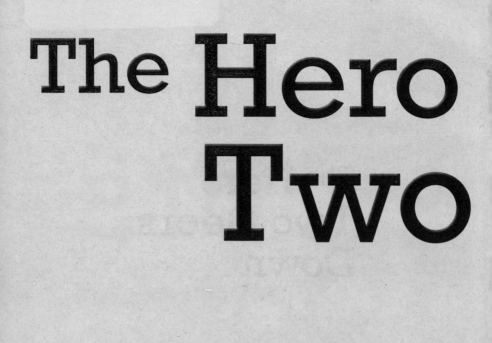

The Hero

Two

Doors Down

Based on the True Story of Friendship between a Boy and a Baseball Legend

SHARON ROBINSON

Scholastic Inc.

To Jessica and Lucas, you are my wings.
And, to our beloved Jesse; we carry you
in our hearts.

This book was originally published in hardcover by Scholastic Press in 2016.

This book is a work of fiction. Names, characters, places, and incidents are either the product of the author's imagination or are used fictitiously, and any resemblance to actual persons, living or dead, business establishments, events, or locales is entirely coincidental.

ISBN 978-0-545-80452-3

10 9 8 7 6   19 20 21

Printed in the U.S.A.   40
First printing 2017
Book design by Abby Dening

PROLOGUE

December 5, 1959, turned out to be the worst day of my life.

I was twenty, a sophomore at Brooklyn College. My dream was to one day become a doctor, so I concentrated on being a good student. But I was also a rebel, and my dad was a prime target. Those boyhood years when my dad and I shared a passion for baseball and the Brooklyn Dodgers were gone. Lately, there was more tension between us than love.

That afternoon the fight was knocked out of me. I came home after a swim meet, tired and hungry. Mom met me at the door, looking worried.

"Stevie, your father's home," Mom said. "He's not feeling well. I'm calling his doctor. Go to him."

If Dad was home in the afternoon, he was really sick. I flew up the stairs. My heart raced as if I was still in the final lap of my last race. When I reached the landing, I was greeted by an eerie silence. It reminded me of a snowstorm that once shut Brooklyn down when I was younger.

I peeked into my parents' bedroom. My dad was propped up against several pillows, struggling to breathe. His eyes were closed and his mouth was open. "Dad," I called out as I rushed to him. I leaned in and shook his shoulders. "Dad?" He sucked in air without speaking. I turned and ran back down the stairs. "Getting an ambulance," I managed as I passed my mother on the steps.

Outside, I felt a burst of cold air on my flushed cheeks. I ran as fast as I could. The fire station on Utica Avenue was only three blocks away. There was always an ambulance parked in front. I reached the open garage. When I saw it was empty, I burst into tears. A fireman came to my rescue. "What's wrong, son?" he asked.

"My dad's in trouble," I gasped between sobs. "We need an ambulance quick!"

"Okay, calm down and tell me what happened," the fireman said.

"He's having trouble breathing. I think it's his heart," I explained.

"Here, write down your name and address," he said, slapping a pad of paper in front of me. "I'll send an ambulance to your house as quickly as possible. Don't panic. You did the right thing for your dad. Now go home and stay there until help arrives."

The restaurants I passed on my way home told a story. A kosher deli, a bagel shop, a Chinese take-out, and a Caribbean restaurant stood side by side. On the opposite side of the street, there was pizza and soul food. Over the years, our mostly Jewish neighborhood had become a community more reflective of the diversity of Brooklyn. "Change is inevitable," Dad would say.

He had spent most of my childhood managing Markell's Shoe Store on Fifth Avenue and 48th Street in Manhattan. Now he made custom shoes for everyone. "When all people, regardless of race or religion, are welcomed in all parts of New York City, from Brooklyn to Manhattan, then we'll defeat discrimination," he'd say at his new shop on Seventh Avenue and 28th Street.

I raced back toward our house. But I was too late.

We buried Dad a couple of days later.

We sat shivah, the Jewish tradition of mourning. All of the mirrors in the house were covered up, and we used boxes to sit on instead of our couches and chairs. Friends and family came over to join us, but I ran away from the talk of Dad in the past tense. I was angry and needed to be alone. I was in no mood to entertain friends. Nothing would bring Dad back. We'd never again press our heads against the transistor radio or watch the news on the black-and-white television in the living room. We'd never work on a car engine or build and fly model airplanes. So what was the point?

I was lying across my bed, thinking of Dad, when my mom walked in with a cardboard box.

"I found this in your father's closet," she said, dropping the box by my bed.

"What is it?" I asked as I lifted up on my right elbow.

"Not sure," Mom replied. "It has your name on it."

I slipped off the bed and settled on the floor beside the box. I lifted the lid and pulled out an envelope addressed to me. It was in my dad's handwriting.

"Oh," Mom said, seeing the note. "Do you want to be alone?"

I shrugged. "I guess."

Mom stood up and slid her fingers through my hair before she left.

The letter was dated December 28, 1957. Two years ago, sometime after we learned that the Brooklyn Dodgers were moving to Los Angeles. It was a particularly rough time for me and Dad.

Steve,
Sorry for the harsh words last night. I woke
up this morning wishing we could end each

battle with a hug. But we're both stubborn and saying "I love you" no longer comes easily. Instead, I preach and punish when I should be telling you how proud you make me. I complain because your bedroom is a mess. Truth is, my own father died when I was young and unprepared. So just in case history strikes twice, I'm trying to prepare you to be a man while you're still young enough to learn.

When I saw you put aside your boyhood treasures, I collected them in this box, knowing that someday you'd find the joy in their reflected memories. Steve, the past often serves as a guide for the future. This box contains some of those clues. I pray you always know how deeply you were loved.

Dad

The note slipped out of my hands and dropped to the floor. I thought of my dad and I sobbed. I remembered him telling me that life wouldn't always give me the answers I wanted. "The storm will pass," he'd said. "Stick close to family, faith, and friendship. They'll help get you through the worst of times, son."

I pushed up on my knees and began to rifle through the box. As I reached inside, the first thing my fingers hit was a ticket stub from the Brooklyn Dodgers 1948 home opener. I stared at the faded paper ticket and thought of how excited I'd been that day. I remembered everything. It made me smile for the first time since Dad died.

CHAPTER 1

The year was 1948. At eight years old, I lived for baseball. The Brooklyn Dodgers was our team. In six weeks, the Dodgers would be back at Ebbets Field. *Maybe this is the year,* I thought as I leapt from the third stair to the landing of our foyer, *that Dad will surprise me with opening day tickets.*

"Good morning, son," Dad greeted me when I walked into the kitchen and slid into my chair.

Mom leaned over and planted a kiss on my forehead. "Good morning."

"I've got good news," Dad said, beaming from behind the *Brooklyn Eagle* newspaper.

"What's that?" I asked.

"Major League Baseball players have reported to spring training," he reported.

"Yippee!" I shouted. "Where are the Dodgers?"

"They're in the Dominican Republic, and Leo Durocher is back as their manager."

"Is that good news? Didn't he get fired?" I remembered something about the Dodgers getting rid of Durocher the year before, though I wasn't sure. I tried to memorize the name of every player and coach on the team, but it wasn't always easy to keep them straight.

Dad chuckled. "Durocher's a good manager whose personal life gets in the way of his success. He was suspended for that last season, but he's served his time and now he gets to come back. Let's hope he learned his lesson," he said.

Even without Leo Durocher as their manager, the Dodgers made it all the way to the World Series last season. It was so exciting until they lost to the Yankees in the seventh game. The whole neighborhood still talked about it. Now a new season was about to start. Could they make it back to the championship?

"How come the Dodgers chose the Dominican Republic for spring training?" I asked.

"The weather's good and the cost of living is low. Besides, Branch Rickey figured the Caribbean would be open to a team with black and white players. But this will be the last year for that. By next year, the Dodgers will have their own training facility in Vero Beach, Florida."

Branch Rickey was a name I knew for sure. Mr. Rickey was the general manager of the Dodgers. He had signed Jackie Robinson last year. It was the first time an African American player had joined a Major League Baseball team. Jackie was a big part of why the Dodgers had won the National League pennant last season.

Dad folded the paper and set it down next to his plate to continue. "According to the *Eagle*, Mr. Rickey is a smart man and his plan is working," he began. "Dodgers fans are showing up in droves to get a good look at Jackie. And in the Dominican Republic, Jackie can stay at the same hotel as his white teammates. Progress, son. We're making progress."

I poured milk into my bowl of cornflakes and spooned Nestlé's Quik into my glass of milk. Before diving in, I looked over at my dad. "Does progress mean that when the Dodgers come home, Jackie will be able to stay in the same hotels as the other Dodgers, like Pee Wee, Gil, Carl, and Ralph Branca?"

"Afraid not, Steve," Dad replied. "There are still laws in the South that keep blacks and whites separated in all public places. We still have a way to go before those laws are broken down. It's not just the South with their Jim Crow laws. There will be hotels in the North and Midwest that will try to keep Jackie out. But the Dodgers will figure a way to keep the team together whenever they can."

Dad paused a moment, then continued. "There's more news that's not so good. Pete Reiser, the Dodgers star outfielder, injured his ankle. After years of serious injuries, they're saying his career is over. Mr. Rickey offered Pete this year off with pay so he could recover, but he refused."

"Pete should listen to Mr. Rickey," I said. "Right, Dad?"

"Maybe, son. Pete's career is on the fence. We'll have to see. Jackie Robinson has some issues, too."

I almost knocked over my chocolate milk. "Jackie?"

"That's right. Even though he won the Rookie of the Year award last season, he showed up at spring training twenty-five pounds overweight this year."

"So he's on a diet?"

"He'll lose weight fast. Durocher's so mad that he called Jackie an old lady. He'll make him run hard and sweat away pounds so fast, Jackie won't need a diet." Dad chuckled.

Poor Jackie, I thought. Daniel, one of my friends, was overweight. Boy, did the kids tease him! I'll never forget the day he ran crying out of school before the last bell. The next day, the principal punished the kids who'd teased Daniel, but I knew it had hurt his feelings.

"But what will happen if Jackie doesn't lose the weight?"

Dad made a mighty grim face. "He'll be fired," he replied.

Fire Jackie! I thought. *Could that really happen?*

After breakfast, I met up with my best friend, Sena, so we could walk the two blocks to P.S. 244, our elementary school.

"The Dodgers started spring training in the Dominican Republic," I announced as soon as our footsteps were in sync.

"That's weird," she replied. "How come they're not in Florida like the Yankees?"

"Because their training facility in Florida isn't finished yet," I explained. Sena was the only kid I knew from Brooklyn who preferred the New York Yankees over the Dodgers. "I'm a little worried about Jackie and Pete Reiser," I added.

"How come?" Sena asked.

"Jackie's overweight, and Pete's injured," I replied.

"They sure better get in shape fast if they have any hopes of beating the Yankees! You know what happened in the World Series last year . . ." Sena declared.

I shot Sena a look. "This year isn't last year. You just wait and see."

"Hey, let's do something fun after school," she said.

"Stickball?" I offered.

"Too cold," Sena replied. "Can you come over to my house and play Scrabble? Mom will make us egg creams. Please?"

"With Fox's U-bet syrup?"

Sena nodded.

"My favorite! I'll check with my mother," I said, my mouth already tasting the mix of chocolate syrup, cream, and soda water.

"You aren't in trouble again, are you?" Sena asked.

"Not exactly, but Miss Maliken sent home another note."

"Let me guess. Missing homework?"

"You got it," I replied. "Luckily, that's all she wrote on the note."

"Is there more?"

"I got in some trouble last week."

"What happened?"

"Not much . . ." I said with a chuckle. "I sat in the last row in music class. The violin section was on break and I was bored. I could tell Josh was, too, so I decided to spice things up. I pulled the cord from the window shade behind Josh and tied it to his pants. When the bell rang, Josh hopped up without realizing he was attached to the cord. His pants ripped open and the whole class saw his underwear. It was hilarious until the window shade began to tear right up the middle."

"Stephen!" Sena shouted.

"Josh turned all red and started screaming at me," I went on. "Kids circled all around us, laughing, while Josh struggled to untie the cord."

"Does this story have a funny ending or a bad one?" Sena asked.

"It's not over," I replied. "The music teacher rushed to the back of the room just as Josh was ready to sock me one. He stepped between us and sent Josh to the principal's office so he could call his mother and get a new pair of pants. I got sent to Miss Maliken. She kept me after school, made me wash blackboards in six classrooms, and gave me a final warning. She was even threatening to go to my house and talk to my parents."

Sena's eyes were wide open. "This could have a very bad ending." Sena groaned. "Two days ago, Robin and I got into a hair-pulling fight on the playground. I think Miss Maliken has had it with me, too."

"Think she'll really go to my house?"

"She might," Sena said.

"Yikes! Bad timing," I told her.

"Because?"

"Baseball season, silly. I'm hoping to go to the Dodgers opener," I replied.

"Then why don't you start doing your homework?" Sena asked.

"I will, and I'll even hand it in on time," I added as we signed off with a pinkie shake and headed to our classrooms.

But the very next day, I got caught playing stickball in the hallway on the third floor. My fate was sealed. Terrified, I waited outside my classroom for Sena. "I've got to talk to you," I told her as soon as she stepped out the door.

"Geez, Steve. What's the emergency?"

"Follow me," I insisted. We crept away from the

rest of the students. "I overheard Miss Maliken tell the principal that she was going to make a home visit."

"Today? To your house?" asked Sena.

"I think so," I replied.

"Maybe we can talk her out of it?"

"How?"

"I'm not sure. But let's wait outside and see what direction Miss Maliken heads when she comes out of the building," Sena said.

"Then what?" I asked.

"If it looks like she's headed toward your house, we stop her."

"I don't think we can convince her not to visit my house."

"You could tell Miss Maliken that your mother is home sick and wouldn't want any company," Sena suggested.

"That's a lie," I said flatly.

"We'll think of something. Just follow my lead," Sena said, yanking my shirt by the collar and pulling me with her.

Scared, we huddled in the shadows of the school building. When our teacher reached the sidewalk, we sprang into action.

"Miss Maliken," I shouted.

"Hey, Miss Maliken," Sena called out.

My teacher stopped a few feet away from us. She was a petite woman, not much taller than Sena and me, but I was intimidated as we approached her. I looked over at Sena for strength. I was surprised to see Sena's hand reaching toward Miss Maliken, but I followed her lead. Together we pushed Miss Maliken, then watched in shock as she toppled over the hedge. The air filled with her screams. I reached over the hedge to help her up but was pushed aside by a dozen mothers and grandmothers who'd come to her aid. Women scrambled to help her. I lost track of Sena while being dragged home by a pack of irate women and my red-faced teacher.

My punishment was swift and harsh. With a ten-day suspension from school and a long list of restrictions at home, I'd ruined my chances of going to the Dodgers opening day.

CHAPTER 2

I knew that pushing my teacher was wrong. And boy, did I pay for it. Ten days of doing extra chores around the house—washing all the dishes and taking out the garbage. Keeping my room clean. I had to make my bed every morning while I was out of school.

The worst part was that I couldn't listen to the radio or ask my dad about how the Dodgers were doing in spring training. It was so boring. I needed to be on my best behavior to have the punishment lifted, so I didn't bother him. I spent most of the time catching up on my missing homework. But I had so many questions. Were they winning? Was Jackie losing the weight? This was torture!

Ten long days later, Dad brought me into the living room.

"Miss Maliken called," he said. "She received your letter of apology and your schoolwork. Your school suspension has been lifted."

"Does that mean I go back to my class in the morning?" I asked. Ten days away from my friends had me missing everything about school.

"They're ready for you, Stephen. The question is . . . are you ready to go back to them?"

"I've learned my lesson," I said.

Dad looked curiously at me. "What lesson is that, son?"

"That I have to be responsible for my behavior and follow the rules," I told him.

"That's an important lesson, Stephen."

"So can I go back to school?"

"You really missed it, didn't you?"

"It's been a long ten days," I admitted.

"You can go back to school tomorrow," Dad said.

"What about at home ... am I still on punishment?"

"No, Stephen, you're not. Your mother and I have been pleased with your willingness to help out at home and your positive attitude. We expect you to keep it up. Same with your school performance. Miss Maliken will give us daily reports. Your school-work is to be done before you go out to play. And you must hand it in on time. Stephen, it's more than just following rules. You must learn to control your impulses or you'll continue to get into trouble. Do you understand me?" Dad asked.

"Sure. I've got to stop acting without thinking about the consequences."

"That's correct," Dad replied.

"I got it, Dad."

"Okay, let's go get some breakfast. Your mother saves making pancakes for special days. I think this qualifies. Don't you?"

"One of the best days . . . next to Dodgers opening day, of course," I replied. "I missed you reading the sports pages to me. Can we talk about the Dodgers while we eat?"

Dad chuckled and wrapped an arm around my shoulder. "You bet. I've missed sharing the news with you."

In between bites of pancakes and slurps of chocolate milk, I peppered Dad with questions. "How's Jackie's weight?"

"It's down," Dad told me. "He still has a way to go."

"Jackie'll do it, Dad. I know he will," I said.

"There's other news . . . Eddie Stanky was traded to Boston. Pete Reiser's looking healthy for the time being, so he's at first base now and Jackie's playing second, where he belongs."

"Gee, Dad . . . did I miss all of spring training?"

"No, but the Dodgers will be finishing up spring training and exhibition games in Vero Beach. After that, they'll barnstorm through some Southern towns."

"Barnstorm? That's when the team travels to a bunch of towns to play practice games, right?"

"That's right. It's a great way for a team to get into shape, playing exhibition games."

"When are they coming home?"

"Late April, son. So we've got time," Dad replied.

"Think we can go to opening day at Ebbets Field?" I asked.

Dad laughed. "Let's see how the next few weeks go before we make any big plans. The Dodgers season is nine months. Certainly we'll make a game or two," Dad said.

"Gotcha," I replied, feeling hopeful. "Can I call Sena and see if she wants to play stickball?"

"If it's okay with your mother," Dad replied.

An hour later, Sena and I, armed with sticks and a Spalding ball, rode our bikes to the school yard. The courts were filled with other boys and girls. We joined a bunch of kids from our school and started up a game. It felt good to be outside playing with friends. We didn't mind the cold air. Actually, it felt good to run around in. I proudly batted with my toes pointed inward like my pigeon-toed hero, Jackie Robinson.

I wasn't the best hitter and I didn't run very fast. So the other kids held out little hope that I'd score.

Still, I swung that wooden stick so hard that it grazed the ball and I got on base. The rest was easier. When I got a chance to run, I'd race around the bases, mustering enough body warmth to keep me going. I was all heart.

Afterward, when we were riding our bikes home, Sena told me that she had heard a black family planned on buying the two-family house at 5224 Tilden Avenue.

"Big deal," I told her.

"My mom said that only Jews should live in our neighborhood," Sena insisted.

"Why's that?" I asked.

"Maybe so we can all go to the same temple?" she suggested. "Or so the neighborhood stays the way it already is?"

I slammed on the brakes and stared back at my friend in disbelief. "I'm going home."

"What's the matter with you?" Sena asked.

"This whole talk makes me mad!" I yelled as I sped away.

"What about a quick game of stoopball?" Sena called.

"Not today," I yelled back at her. I didn't understand my sudden anger, but I knew it had to do with what my friend had said. All I could think of was how hard Jackie had fought his first season with the Dodgers just because his skin was black. Players and fans tried to make Jackie quit so they could keep baseball a white man's game. Jackie fought back with a well-timed base steal and a mighty swing.

I reached home, hot and frustrated. I stomped through the kitchen and grabbed a quick snack on my way into my room. Trying to make sense of my feelings, I pulled out the tin can that held my most precious baseball cards. I separated them so the Dodgers starting lineup was on top. Jackie was in the mix. *Could Brooklyn win the World Series without him? Could they even get back there if he wasn't on the team?* I wondered. I skimmed Jackie's statistics for his rookie year. He'd batted .297, scored 125 runs, and stole 29 bases. His great play was a big part of the Dodgers making it last year. "Pretty impressive," I muttered. I studied his rookie card before slipping it back on top of the heap—he was the Rookie of the Year, that doesn't come easy.

Over dinner, I told my father what Sena had said.

Dad leaned in toward me until our foreheads touched. "Son, that's nonsense and flat-out prejudice," he said.

Mom walked into the dining room as we were talking. She set the platter of baked chicken and boiled potatoes mixed with carrots in the middle of the table and joined the conversation.

"Some of those same neighbors brought a petition by for your dad and me to sign. It said that they objected to the sale of 5224 Tilden Avenue to a Negro family. I started to tear it up, but ripped into the lady instead," Mom said.

"What'd you say to her, Ma?" I asked.

"I told her that no Jew should sign that petition."

I folded my hands in my lap and played thumb wrestle. I was worried. If they didn't want Negroes in the neighborhood, they wouldn't want them to play baseball, either. Could this petition get Jackie kicked off the team?

"How come?" I asked.

"Let's finish this conversation after dinner," Mom suggested.

Dad led us in prayer and then we ate.

I was starving, so I dove into my meal, tearing the tender brown meat off the leg and thigh bones. A tense silence filled the air—my stack of baseball cards was all I could think about. I knew Jackie's staying with the Dodgers and Negroes' moving onto my block were connected. But how?

When my belly was full, I peered up at my dad. I wanted to lift the mood in our dining room. He smiled over at me and I sighed. Maybe the news wasn't all bad.

I watched as Dad pushed his plate a few inches forward. He cleared his throat. "Prejudice, Steve, is when you judge a person based on the color of their skin or their religion and not by their character. Prejudice leads to discrimination."

"Like what happened with Jackie during spring training when the Dodgers had to play in the Dominican Republic so that they could all stay in the same hotel?" I asked.

"Exactly," Dad replied. "You won't remember this, Steve, but in 1946, Jackie trained with a Dodgers farm team, the Montreal Royals, in Florida. The hotels refused to let Jackie stay with the team because he was a black man. Instead, he stayed in private homes in the black community."

"That's not fair," I said.

"Exactly, son. That's why Branch Rickey had the 1947 Dodgers train in Cuba and this year he brought them to the Dominican Republic. The color of their skin kept black and Latin players out of Major League Baseball for many years, until last year when Jackie Robinson broke the color barrier. Still, there are a number of baseball teams that are hesitant to field a black and white team. Well, there is also discrimination in neighborhoods. Families who are a different race or come from foreign countries or are Jewish are not welcome and cannot buy or rent an apartment or a house in certain communities. Prejudice and discrimination are wrong, son. Our family will not discriminate against another person."

I smiled, feeling proud of my Dodgers and my family. "So how come Sena's mother wants to keep a black family out of our neighborhood?" I asked.

"Stevie"—my mother stepped in—"we don't know that Sena's mother is prejudiced. This neighborhood has been all Jewish for years. Sena's mom may have been explaining to Sena why some of our neighbors were afraid of changing our neighborhood."

"Your mother's right. We can only speak for ourselves. This household remembers how horribly history has treated people of the Jewish faith. That knowledge makes us opposed to any kind of discrimination."

"What do you mean?" I asked my dad.

"Do you remember that your bubbe and zayde, my parents, left Russia for America when they were in their twenties?"

"Sure," I said. "They still talk with accents."

"They fled Russia, along with two million other Jewish families, hoping to find freedom to practice their religion, live wherever they want, send their children to school, and get a job to support their families," my father explained.

"In Russia, Jews were treated very badly," my mother added. "There was a lot of violence against them, and many men, women, and children were hurt or killed simply because they were Jewish. They were forced to give up their homes, close down their synagogues, and live in overcrowded conditions in extreme poverty. Russian Jews could not get jobs and their children had limited access to education. So they escaped these terrible conditions in hopes of providing a better life for their families. This happened a long time ago. Long before you or your father and I were born. Your grandparents had the courage to immigrate to the United States."

"That's right, Steve," my father said. "Because of their courage, we now have a better life, but not one that is free of prejudice or discrimination. Some of our neighbors are afraid that opening the neighborhood to people of different faiths, cultures, and races will somehow threaten their way of life. Your mother and I don't feel this way. We believe in freedom for all people regardless of race, religion, or culture. We welcome families of different faiths and races into our community."

"That's why we didn't sign the petition," Mom said. "It could have prevented a Negro family from buying a house in this neighborhood. We didn't agree."

I sat for a minute trying to put their words together. I sort of understood but could only make sense of it in baseball terms. "Jackie Robinson is one of the best players the Dodgers have ever had, black or white. And now the Dodgers will finally win a

World Series. Everyone will see what Jackie can do," I stated firmly.

"That's a good analogy, son. Some people wanted to keep baseball all white. But after Jackie's rookie year and the Dodgers' success, they've learned a lesson. We're stronger and better when we don't judge people by the color of their skin or their religion. And, together, we *will* make a winning team."

I beamed.

As far as I could tell, Jackie Robinson was safe for now.

CHAPTER 3

The next day, Sena pulled me aside. "Still mad at me?" she asked.

"Not really," I replied.

"Good, because I took some money from my piggy bank so we can stop by the candy store and get milk shakes."

"Sounds good to me," I said. "I can't stay long, though."

"Me either," Sena replied.

We walked over to the Jenkins Candy Shoppe in silence.

"I wasn't really mad at you. I was just mad," I told Sena as we climbed up on leather-covered bar stools and ordered two vanilla shakes.

Sena looked embarrassed. "My dad was pretty mad, too. Especially when Mom told him that some of the neighbors sent around a paper asking people to sign up saying that they didn't want Negroes in our neighborhood. Mom told me that some of our neighbors were afraid of change. She admitted that was her first reaction, too, but she understands now that we can't be afraid of change or judge someone else based on their differences from us."

"We had the same talk at my house," I said. "My parents refused to sign that paper. I'd hate for the Dodgers to go back to an all-white team."

"Yeah. Jackie's brought so much excitement to Brooklyn," Sena agreed.

"True. Since Jackie's joined the Dodgers, two other teams have signed Negro players. Cleveland brought Larry Doby to the Indians. Hank Thompson plays for the St. Louis Browns. And now Mr. Rickey's talking about moving their top catcher prospect, Roy Campanella, up from the Minors."

"Think he'll make it in time for opening day?" Sena asked.

"I sure hope so," I said.

"Will you be there?"

"I heard Dad tell my mother that he had to work," I muttered.

"My father has opening day tickets taped to the refrigerator. It's all he talks about," Sena said.

"Is he taking you?" I asked.

"Are you kidding? I'm the only one in the family

who's a Yankees fan. Dad wouldn't waste his money taking me to a Dodgers game."

I laughed. "Maybe you'll get to go when the Dodgers beat the Yankees in the World Series."

"Keep dreaming," Sena replied.

We finished our milk shakes and raced each other to my front porch. Sena won by a foot. Embarrassed, I challenged her to a do-over and beat her! I was glad we could put our fight behind us.

Later, I was upstairs in my room finishing math homework when my father peeked in the doorway. "Hi, son," he greeted me. His face had a wide grin plastered across it as if he had a secret.

"Hey, Dad," I called out, studying a man who usually wasn't so cheerful after work.

"I have good news," Dad said, venturing inside my room.

"You got us opening day tickets?"

"No, Stephen. I do not have opening day tickets," Dad replied.

Maybe we really *weren't going to the Dodgers opener*, I thought. My father sat on the edge of my bed.

"Sorry to disappoint you, but my news may cheer you up. You remember we talked about a black family buying 5224 Tilden Avenue?"

"Yeah, I remember."

"Well, the sale went through. The Palin family will move in soon."

"What about that piece of paper and the neighbors not wanting a Negro family to move in?"

"Turns out that only a couple of people signed the petition," Dad explained. "Most of our neighbors feel as your mother and I do. The Palins should not have any trouble from the neighbors. They will be welcome."

"Is that the good news?" I asked.

"Part of it," Dad replied. "The real estate agent who sold the house to the Palins is a customer of mine at the shoe store. He came in today and told me that the Palins have rented the top floor of their house to a player from the Dodgers!"

I jumped up from my desk chair and faced my father. *"Are you kidding?"* I'd heard that players lived in regular Brooklyn neighborhoods, but I'd never dreamed I'd be so lucky to have one live near me. "Who is it, Dad?"

"That's the thing," my father said. "My friend said he wasn't at liberty to share that information. I think they're waiting until the lease is signed. So I guess we'll just have to wait and see."

"Aw," I sighed. "Gee, Dad . . . do you think it's Pee Wee?"

Dad stood up. "I don't know."

"Jackie?"

"Stephen, stop guessing. We'll know soon."

I couldn't sleep that night. I stayed awake thinking about my new neighbors. I knew that when the baseball season was over, players usually returned to their home communities so they could work. At the start of the season, they had to find a new place to rent closer to their teams. Some players shared rooms in private homes and walked to work at Ebbets Field. So it could be any of the players.

At breakfast, I pressed Dad for more details. "Since the Palins are Negroes, it makes sense that they'd rent to a black family. So it's either the Robinsons or maybe Roy Campanella."

"That's a possibility, but just because the Palins are Negroes doesn't mean their tenant will be black," Dad reminded me.

"True, but you have to admit it's likely," I pressed.

"The Dodgers have forty players on their roster. It could be any of those men."

"I bet you it's Jackie," I announced, jumping up from the table and dancing around the kitchen, shouting, "Jackie! Jackie! Jackie!"

"Sit down, Stephen," Dad commanded. "You're getting ahead of yourself. And don't go to school bragging that Jackie Robinson is moving to Tilden Avenue."

"Really . . . Dad? A Dodgers player two doors down. I don't care who it is," I said. "This is a dream come true."

He chuckled. "I understand, son."

The next couple of weeks were absolute torture. In late March, a moving van pulled up in front of 5224. I ran out of the house without a jacket and plopped down on the top step. I watched as the Palin family's furniture was unloaded from the truck and hauled into the bottom floor. As evening set in, Mom called me inside for dinner.

"The new family has moved in," I reported.

"Yes, I saw the van. Did you see any children?"

"A boy and girl, but they look like teenagers," I told her.

"Is that why you look so disappointed?" Mom asked.

"I was hoping it was the ballplayer's moving van."

"It shouldn't be much longer, Steve. I'm planning on cooking a pot roast and taking it over to Mrs. Palin tomorrow. Want to come with me?"

"Sure," I replied. "Think Mrs. Palin will tell us who's going to be living on the top floor?"

"I don't know, Stephen. And you are not to bring it up. We're going over there to welcome the Palins to the neighborhood, not pry into their private business," Mom scolded.

"But, Mom . . ." I moaned.

"Whoever moves into 5224 obviously wants privacy. They have to deal with fans at the ballpark. When they come home, they're family men just like your dad. He'll want time for his family. You will have to respect that, Stephen. Am I clear?"

"Yes, Mom. I won't be a pest," I promised.

The next morning, we walked over to greet our new neighbors. It was cold, but I was sweating under my jacket. Would Mrs. Palin tell us who was renting her top floor? Would I be disappointed if it was an unknown player? Or would I get the best news of my life?

Mrs. Palin opened the door on the first ring.

"Good morning," Mom began. "My name is Sarah Satlow and this is my son, Stephen. We are your neighbors. We wanted to welcome you to Tilden Avenue."

"How lovely and unexpected," Mrs. Palin proclaimed. "It's nice to meet you both. My name is Elinor Palin. Stephen, you'll see my children around the neighborhood. They're a bit older than you and go to Tilden High School. You must be at the elementary school, right?"

"Yes, Mrs. Palin," I replied politely.

"We know how chaotic it is to move, so I baked a pot roast for you and your family," Mom said, handing Mrs. Palin a covered pan, still warm, along with brownies wrapped in wax paper.

"It smells divine," Mrs. Palin said. "Thank you."

Sweat dripped down my neck. Should I risk making my mother angry by asking Mrs. Palin about her future tenant? Or should I keep quiet?

"Are you a Brooklyn Dodgers fan, Stephen?" Mrs. Palin asked.

"I'm a big fan," I replied, relieved that she brought up the subject.

"Who are your favorite players?"

"Jackie and Pee Wee are my top two. But I also like Ralph Branca and Carl Erskine. Why?"

"Just curious," Mrs. Palin replied, with a twinkle in her eye.

"But—" I started to push, then looked up at my mom and shut my mouth.

"I know there's a rumor that one of the Dodgers is moving in upstairs," Mrs. Palin said.

I nodded.

"Well, Stephen. My husband made me promise not to tell anyone who our tenant is going to be. So we'll all just have to wait to see who moves in," Mrs. Palin said with a warm smile.

I almost fell to the ground and screamed out in frustration. Not another person telling me to wait. No, I couldn't stand it! I barely heard my mother say good-bye. Tears in my eyes, I followed her back to our house.

I trudged up the stairs, feeling mad. "Why didn't she tell us?"

"For all the reasons we discussed earlier," Mom said.

"I still think it's Jackie."

That night I was sitting on the front stoop when Dad came home from work. He saw me staring down the block at our new neighbor's house.

"Your mother told me you met the Palins today."

"Yes." I nodded.

"I've been debating about when was the right time to tell you this," Dad said.

"Tell me what?"

"I now know who is renting from the Palins," he replied.

"Who is it, Dad? You've got to tell me. Please?" I begged.

"Until they move in, we won't know for sure," Dad teased.

"Is it who I've been wishing for?"

Dad chuckled. "I think you'll be very happy," he said.

"Dad, are you telling me that Jackie Robinson is going to be my neighbor?"

He beamed. "I saw Mr. Palin today. He told me that Jackie and his family have signed the lease for April first."

I couldn't believe it! Jackie Robinson! I jumped into Dad's arms, yelling with joy. But Dad's laughter worried me. It was almost April 1 and he loved a good April Fool's joke. I pulled away from him. "Are you making up a story?"

"I wouldn't do that to you, son."

"Is it *really* true, Dad?"

"It's true, son. Mr. Palin said that Mrs. Robinson is driving their Cadillac across country with her brother, Raymond, and little Jackie Junior. They're expected in New York sometime between April fifth and seventh—"

"What about Jackie?"

"He's still barnstorming with the team, Steve."

"Oh, yeah. That's right. Is Jackie Junior my age?" I asked.

"I think he's younger than you. You'll know soon," Dad replied.

"I'll bet they'll be here tomorrow. Can I stay home from school?"

"I'm not even going to respond to that question, Steve."

I laughed it off. "All right, Dad, but will you come get me out of school the minute the moving van pulls up?"

"No," my dad said. "I'll be at work and you'll be at school. You've got to give the Robinsons privacy, Steve. Promise me you won't drive Mrs. Robinson crazy with questions about Jackie."

I slid down to the step below my dad. I honestly didn't know how I'd react to Jackie Robinson's living so close to me. It was just too important. None of my friends would even believe me until Jackie actually moved in. I looked up at my dad and shrugged my shoulders. "I'll try not to be a pest," I promised.

I jumped off the stoop. "Time me," I insisted before racing to Jackie Robinson's new house and back. "How long did that take, Dad?"

"Thirty seconds, tops," Dad said.

"Just think, I'll be living that close to a Brooklyn Dodgers player!" I shouted.

Every day after school, Sena and I would race home hoping to find a moving van parked outside of 5224 Tilden Avenue. Wednesday, April 7, I got my wish. We broke into a trot, reaching the truck just as two men lifted an off-white couch from the back of the van.

My heart pounded so hard I was sure the men would see it beating under my coat. I wanted so badly to peek inside the house, but Sena wouldn't let go of my hand. Instead, we stood back and watched for a glimpse of the Robinson family.

We stood out there for what felt like forever without seeing anyone.

Finally, Sena had to get back home. I knew my mom wouldn't want me to be out there trying to see the Robinsons, so I headed home, too.

This wait was driving me crazy! I kicked a small stone in frustration as I walked toward my stoop.

"There's a moving truck outside the Robinsons'," I reported as soon as I got inside and Mom shut the door.

"I know, honey."

We sat in the kitchen snacking on crisp carrots

and apple juice. I was antsy to get back outside and continue looking for our new neighbors. "Can I ride my bike?"

"You promised your father that you wouldn't pester the Robinsons," Mom reminded me.

"I just want to make sure it's them. That's all," I protested.

"Move-in day is stressful. Give them space. Saturday, we can pick cherry blossoms and bring them over to Mr. and Mrs. Robinson. How does that sound?"

"Fine," I muttered. "I'll just sit on the stoop."

"You may not leave the yard," my mother told me.

"I won't."

I sat on the top step until the workmen brought the last piece of furniture into the house. I spotted Mrs. Robinson and her son once, but there was no sign of Jackie. I was being cool and staying at a safe distance from the Robinsons' home. But I couldn't guarantee how I'd react when Jackie appeared. My stomach was in knots. I almost cried when the moving van pulled away from the curb and Mom called me inside.

Saturday morning, I was up before sunrise. I opened my bedroom window and stuck my head out. I stayed there until Mom pulled me back inside.

"Stephen," she scolded. "How many times do I have to tell you not to lean out of the window?"

"Oh, Ma . . . I was just looking for Jackie."

"Get dressed. After breakfast, we'll pick some cherry blossoms from the tree in our front yard and take them over to the Robinsons' house."

I jumped into my mother's arms, kissing her generously on both cheeks. She hugged me tight. "Thank you, Mom."

Chuckling, my mother reminded me that Jackie might still be traveling. "Try not to show your disappointment, Steve."

I looked up at her, wondering how to pull that off.

CHAPTER 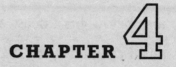 4

All this waiting to catch sight of Jackie was wearing on me. He'd been my favorite player since Dad announced that I was old enough to start listening to Dodgers games with him on the radio. That was on my eighth birthday last June, during Jackie's rookie season. Dad said that would make me into a true Dodgers fan! Then maybe I could go see a game live at Ebbets Field.

I'll never forget it. It was a warm Brooklyn summer night. Mom agreed that Dad and I could have dinner on the stoop. She fixed us a picnic meal of fried chicken, French fries, salad, and Kool-Aid. We ate with the small transistor radio between our plates. Dad sat on the top step. I took my position just below his knees. We turned the radio up loud and I chewed softly. I didn't dare talk.

By the time the game got under way, the porches of our neighbors were filled with eager Dodgers fans. A few women were scattered in folding chairs, supervising as kids played on the sidewalk. Part of me wanted to play, but my father's voice kept pulling me back to the game.

"Jackie Robinson is a rookie, Steve," Dad said. "The Dodgers are in first place and drawing big crowds to Ebbets Field. Jackie's got a lot to do with that. He's batting over .300 and has four homers so far. He's been hit six times by pitchers and been insulted plenty just because he's a black man in a previously all-white game. Jackie hasn't let the pressure get to him. The whole country knows about Brooklyn now. We're special. That's something to be proud of, son."

Dad stopped talking right when the announcer introduced Jackie. Then he said softly so we wouldn't miss a second of Jackie's at-bat, "Listen closely now, Stevie. You'll hear what I'm talking about."

I bent down until my right ear practically touched the plastic box. Jackie's hit got him on base, and within minutes he was threatening the pitcher from third base. *Boy, is he fast*, I thought.

"Jackie Robinson takes a large lead off third base, waits for the Pirates' Fritz Ostermueller to take the full windup, and breaks for home!"

I sat up straight. Tension permeated the hot air. I fixed my gaze on my dad's face, seeing the joy in it as Jackie stole home base for the first time in his Major League Baseball career! Dad jumped to his feet and lifted me high into the air. Our screams of joy were echoed throughout the neighborhood. At that moment, I knew Jackie Robinson was my guy!

That was a year earlier. Since then, I'd read Jackie's book, *My Own Story*, and studied his baseball cards until I was an expert on Jackie's first year in baseball. The 1947 Dodgers were the first time that a racially mixed team ever played in the championship.

Now with the 1948 season looming, I wondered how Jackie would do this year. More important, I looked over at the house where Jackie was set to live, I wondered what he was *really* like. The closer I came to actually meeting Jackie Robinson, the more I worried that I'd be disappointed. I really wanted to like him and to have Jackie like me. But what if he was too busy to notice me? Or what if he saw me and didn't care to get to know me better? Was it even possible for a boy to have a famous man as a friend? I was driving myself nuts trying to figure out who Jackie was, so I decided to ask my mother.

"Mom, do you think Jackie's nice?"

We were cleaning up my room. Mom stopped vacuuming the rug and looked over at me. "I guess so," she said. "He's definitely a strong and courageous man."

"And a great baseball player," I added. "He's gonna play second base this year. Dad says that's his best position. I can't wait to go to Ebbets Field to see Jackie and Pee Wee work together."

"Your father told me last night that the Dodgers opening game is on April twentieth against the Giants. The Dodgers home opener is April twenty-third," Mom said.

"That's less than two weeks away!" I exclaimed. "Think Dad will take me to the Dodgers home opener?"

"Not sure, Stephen. But keep up your good behavior at home and school and anything is possible," Mom replied.

"I'm doing my best," I said.

"Yes, you are," Mom agreed. "Now put on your shoes and come down to the kitchen for breakfast."

I followed my mother to the kitchen. Dad was already at the table with his newspaper in hand. We ate together. Since it was Saturday, I didn't have school, but my father had to work. Saturdays were Dad's busiest day. Mom and I were walking Dad to the stoop when I had an idea.

"Dad, you make and sell custom shoes, right?"

"That's right, son."

"Do you think you could make a special shoe for Jackie? I bet he'd like that! A cleat that would protect him in case a mean player tried to spike him again." Dad told me once that players often slid into second base with their cleats pointing forward. It was dangerous and could lead to a serious injury for the second baseman. I didn't want to see Jackie get hurt!

"You know, Steve, that is a wonderful idea," Dad said as he waved good-bye.

Mom and I picked the brightest cherry blossoms off the giant tree in our front yard. It was still too early to drop by the Robinsons, so we sat at the kitchen table and read the *Archie* comic strip. Mom and her friends liked the love triangle between Archie, Betty, and Veronica. I liked all the crazy things Jughead would do.

While we cleaned up the kitchen, Mom chatted on and on about Mrs. Robinson. I could tell she was nervous about meeting a famous woman.

"You know, Steve, I admire Mrs. Robinson as much as you do her husband. She's so elegant and beautiful."

I was a bit surprised that my mother had paid such close attention to Mrs. Robinson. I'd never heard her talk about any of the other Dodgers wives.

"She and Jackie met in college," Mom added. "I read a story about them in the *Brooklyn Eagle* last year. University of California, wasn't it?"

"Jackie lettered in four sports at UCLA in just one year," I answered. "He was a famous athlete even before he joined the Dodgers. I read his biography."

"And Mrs. Robinson is a nurse, just like me."

"Mom, it's after ten," I whined. I was impatient to meet our new neighbors. "Can we go?"

I was blown away when Mrs. Robinson opened their door and smiled down at me. *She is pretty*, I thought. *And nice.* A little boy clung to her leg.

"I'm Sarah Satlow and this is my son, Stephen. We live two doors down and wanted to welcome you to the neighborhood," Mom said.

"How nice of you," Mrs. Robinson replied. "I'm Rachel and this is my son. Jackie's a little shy right now, but give him a few minutes and he'll want to play. How old are you, Stephen?"

"I turn nine in June," I said, then peeked around Mrs. Robinson so I could see into the living room. There was no sign of Jackie Senior.

"Jackie is almost two and a half," Mrs. Robinson told me.

"Steve and I picked these from our tree for you," Mom said, handing Mrs. Robinson the bouquet of flowers.

"They're lovely! Thank you, Sarah and Steve," Rachel said.

"Is Jackie—"

"Stephen!" Mom scolded me.

"I mean, Mr. Robinson at home?" I asked.

Mrs. Robinson chuckled. "No, Steve. But I'll tell him that you stopped by. Are you a Dodgers fan?"

"You bet!"

"Great! Would you like to go to a game with little Jackie and me this summer?"

"You've got to be kidding? Would I ever!" If I couldn't go to the Dodgers opening home game with Dad, at least I'd be able to go to a game with Mrs. Robinson. *Pretty cool*, I thought.

"I'm serious as long as your parents give you permission," Mrs. Robinson replied.

"Please forgive my son, Rachel. Steve and my husband, Archie, share a deep love for the Dodgers and for your husband. He's thrilled to meet you and a bit too excited to have you as a neighbor," my mother explained.

"I can imagine," Mrs. Robinson said, then gave me another warm smile. "Jack and I love children, Sarah. You don't have to apologize. I'd invite you inside, but we're still unpacking boxes."

"Of course. I understand completely. It was lovely to meet you," my mother said, tapping me with her elbow.

"Nice to meet you," I echoed.

"Thank you for the warm welcome and beautiful flowers," Mrs. Robinson said. "We'll see you soon."

I was totally disappointed and didn't feel like pretending. My head was hanging low as we left the Robinsons' front yard. All I could think of was, would I *ever* meet Jackie Robinson?

Every day during the two weeks leading up to the Dodgers opening game, I woke up thinking this would be it. I decided that the only way I'd spot Jackie Robinson coming out of his house was to be visible. I came up with a plan.

On Monday morning, I got up at six, dressed for school, and had breakfast with my dad at seven o'clock. That left me with an hour before school to spot Jackie. I parked myself on our stoop, read the sports page, and kept my eyes on the redbrick house two doors down.

After school, I played stoopball and finished my homework outside. Waiting and hoping Jackie would come home while I was outside. No luck. Days passed without a single sighting.

"I can't believe he's two doors down and I haven't bumped into him!" I vented to Sena on our walk home from school one afternoon.

"Stephen Jay Satlow, give it a rest!" Sena shouted at me.

I was shocked. Didn't she get it? He was my hero. He was my neighbor. Spotting Jackie Robinson was the only goal. Speaking directly to him would be a bonus. My whole life depended on a handshake. A wave of the cap. Hearing Jackie say my name. "Oh, Sena," I replied in disgust. "If you weren't a Yankees fan, you'd get it."

The Hero Two Doors Down

The closer we got to the home opener, the more obsessed I became. The Robinson family had lived in the neighborhood almost two weeks and I still hadn't spotted Jackie.

The next thing I knew, it was April 20—opening day! The Dodgers were opening the season on the road. Dad and I sat on the front porch listening to the first game of the 1948 season. The Dodgers were playing their crosstown rivals, the New York Giants, at the Polo Grounds. With Jackie on second and the newly acquired catcher, Roy Campanella, at home plate, the Dodgers were once again making history. They were now the first Major League team to have two black players in the regular lineup. It was a three-game series at the Giants' stadium. By the end, the Dodgers took two out of three games.

Friday, April 23, our beloved Brooklyn Dodgers returned to Ebbets Field! Their home opener was against the Philadelphia Phillies at two in the afternoon. I begged Dad not to send me to school. I simply had to stay home and listen to the game on the radio.

"Please, please, please, Dad," I pleaded.

He looked up from his plate of scrambled eggs and wheat toast and smiled at me. "Got a surprise for you, son."

I sat up straight in my chair. "What is it, Dad?" I asked.

While my curiosity mounted, my father toyed with the saltshaker, then reached into his pocket and pulled out two tickets. He handed them to me and I jumped out of my seat!

"This is unbelievable! I thought you'd forgotten. Or didn't want to go. Dad, I'm the happiest kid in Brooklyn." I leaned in and kissed my father on his cheek.

"You've worked hard to improve your attitude

at school and home," Dad said. "Miss Maliken's reports are all good. And I wanted to share this special day with you."

"I've never been so excited!" I told my father. "Maybe now I'll finally meet Jackie Robinson. Think so, Dad?"

"I don't know, son. It's possible."

"Mrs. Robinson said that Jackie liked children," I told him. "Maybe he'll come over to me after batting practice and I can get him to sign my baseball," I said.

"If you meet Jackie Robinson, I imagine he'll sign your ball."

"Can we go early?"

"That's the plan," Dad said with a chuckle.

Dad and I took the train to Ebbets Field for five cents. On the ride there, I rehearsed my first words to Jackie. I turned the new baseball in my hands. I'd planned on meeting Jackie in our neighborhood, but it didn't matter. If I saw him, I'd tell him that we're neighbors. That would be just as good.

"Dad, were the tickets very expensive?" I asked.

"It was worth every penny. I don't know when you've been this happy."

"I am happy, Dad. I will remember this day always," I said, leaning in and hugging his shoulder. "Thank you so, so much!" I looked away. My smile was mixed with tears in my eyes, and I didn't want my father to see them. I went back to rehearsing what I'd say when I met Jackie Robinson. "I live two doors down from you," I repeated softly. Yes, that would make me different from all the other kids. Or I could just say, "I'm your neighbor." Yes, I decided. That was simpler.

We reached our train stop and exited in the direction of Ebbets Field. "Let's wait here, son," Dad said. We stopped by a side gate of the stadium.

"Why are we stopping here?" I asked, wanting to go inside the stadium and make my way down to the field so I could get autographs.

"I'm meeting someone," my father replied.

"But, Dad . . ." I moaned. "I'm going to miss batting practice." I tossed my baseball into the air and caught it. As we waited, I threw the ball higher and higher before getting bored. "Dad . . ." I pleaded.

"Patience, son."

"What time is it?"

My father looked at his watch. "It's noon," he reported. "The game doesn't start until two."

"What time does batting practice end?"

"Our team warms up last. That should be around twelve thirty," Dad replied. "We've got time."

I kicked the stadium wall hard, then remembered that Ebbets Field was old and fragile. At least that's what everyone was saying. It had been built in 1913 right in the middle of the neighborhood. The stands were so close to the field, you could hear players talking to each other and see the expressions on their faces. But now they needed a new stadium. I wondered if they'd knock Ebbets Field down and build a new one in the same spot.

"Gee, Dad," I said after we'd been standing outside the park for what seemed like a very long time. "I'll never get any autographs here. We need to be inside near the bullpen like the other kids."

"In a minute."

"You keep saying that, but we're wasting time. Let's go. Please," I pleaded unsuccessfully. Frustrated, I turned away from my father. When I turned back around, Dad was grinning. I looked around again and spotted two men walking fast and right toward us. "Dad!" I said. "How'd this happen?"

"What?"

"I think it's Jackie and Roy Campanella," I said.

"So it is," Dad replied.

"Are they coming to meet us?" Could this be possible? Had my father made this happen, too? My heart pounded against my chest so hard it frightened me. I was frantic. The moment I'd been waiting for had arrived and I couldn't think of anything to say.

My father grabbed my hand. "Let's go, Steve. I know this is what you've wanted."

We closed the gap between the famous ballplayers and ourselves. I looked up at my hero and my mind went blank. I stood frozen.

"Steve," Jackie said, extending his hand toward me.

My eyeballs nearly popped out of their sockets. *He knows my name?* I reached out and took Jackie's hand. No words came to mind or out of my mouth. I just stared like a starstruck kid.

"Thank you for the cherry blossoms. They looked great on our dining room table," Jackie said easily, like we were friends already. "My wife tells me that you're one of our biggest fans." My head bobbed, but I still couldn't speak. For weeks, I'd played this very scene over and over, and now that Jackie was standing in front of me, I balked. In my head, questions collided and disappeared. I couldn't speak.

"I'd like you to meet Roy Campanella," Jackie said to me.

Again, I dropped the ball and nodded at Roy instead of speaking. Forcing a smile, I stared up at these two great men, hoping they'd understand.

"I'm afraid you've rendered my usually talkative son speechless, Mr. Robinson," Dad said as he stepped in to fill the void. "I'm Archie, Steve's dad. This is such a thrill! My son has been on neighborhood watch for weeks hoping to catch a glimpse of you. He was rehearsing his first greeting up until a few seconds ago. Guess all the practice fogged up his head."

I listened intently as my dad talked baseball with Jackie and Roy. He made it look so easy, I couldn't even get my own name to come out of my mouth! Jackie turned away from my father and looked directly at me.

"Now that we have a few home games, you'll be seeing me around," he said.

I smiled. If words wouldn't come out, at least I could get my mouth to do that. I handed Jackie my baseball and watched as he and Roy signed it. "Thank you," I whispered when the autographed ball was back in my hand.

My dad shook hands with the ballplayers and wished them a successful season.

"Steve, Roy and I have to get inside for batting practice. Why don't you drop by the house sometime? My son would get a kick out of having a big boy to play with."

"Okay," I whispered.

"Thank you," Dad replied.

I looked over at my dad. He'd set this up just for me. But how?

When Jackie turned to leave, I called out, "What should I call you?"

Jackie flashed me a smile that would warm the North Pole. "Call me Jackie."

CHAPTER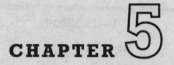

Dad and I maneuvered our way through crowds down to the field. We stood among hundreds of fans who were cheering on their favorite players taking batting practice. I looked over the faces in the crowd when Jackie got up to take his practice swings. They burst into loud cheering when he hit his third homer in a row!

"Did you see that, Dad?" I shouted over the roar of the crowd.

"Sure did, son. Roy's up next," he replied.

We welcomed our new catcher by screaming, "Roy! Roy! Roy!" He rewarded us with a solid line drive that hit the outfield wall.

"Hit it higher," I screamed, hoping for a home run the next swing.

As batting practice wound down, players made their way over to the crowd to sign baseballs. I leaned over the wall, extended my arms toward the players, and called out to my favorite stars. Pee Wee, Duke Snider, and Ralph Branca signed the same ball as Jackie and Roy. By the time Dad and I took our seats, my heart was racing. The game hadn't even started yet and it was already my best day ever!

I handed Dad my signed ball. "Please put it away for me, Dad. I want to save it forever!"

Dad slid my precious baseball into his jacket pocket. "Don't worry, son. I'll keep it safe."

The Hero Two Doors Down

More than 25,000 fans attended the season home opener. My eyes filled with tears as we all stood to sing the national anthem. Many of the Dodgers fans stayed on their feet to boo the Phillies lineup. But the stadium rocked with cheers when the Brooklyn Dodgers players were announced.

A few minutes later the crowd roared again when a padded Roy Campanella came out of the dugout and squatted behind home plate. Campanella caught a few warm-up pitches from the Dodgers starter, Joe Hatten, until finally the announcer yelled, "Let's play ball!"

The crowd's energy could be felt throughout the stands. Our Dodgers were back! I looked around in amazement. I was so pumped up, it was hard to settle into my seat. At each new roar from a section of the crowd, I jumped up to see what was happening.

Across the park was the Dodgers Sym-Phony—a group of fans with instruments who played off-key as fans gathered around, cheering them on. No one minded that they didn't sound like a real symphony. If an umpire made a questionable call, the Sym-Phony played "Three Blind Mice," which sent laughter from one side of the park to the other.

"This is *so* much better than listening to the game on the radio," I said, giddy with anticipation. *What was going to happen next?* Just as I thought that, Philadelphia's base runner, Richie Ashburn, stole home. The Phillies were off to a strong start.

"You're right. There's nothing like Ebbets Field."

Jackie Robinson was the first Dodger up to bat.

"Hit a homer, Jackie!" I yelled with all my might.

Jackie singled to the shortstop. Next, Arky Vaughan popped out and Preston Ward struck out.

I was still cheering for Jackie when he was caught on an attempted steal. I wasn't worried. It was only the first inning.

"Did you notice that Branch Rickey padded the outfield wall?" my father asked me as the Dodgers took to the field.

"Um," I murmured, looking toward the outfield wall. "I see it now."

"Mr. Rickey did that to prevent another Pete Reiser injury," Dad said.

As the game progressed, I paid close attention to Jackie and Pee Wee Reese. Jackie had only just moved to second base at the start of this season. With Pee Wee at shortstop, they had to work together. I watched closely as the two talked to each other while turning a beautiful double play.

Jackie was at bat three times and got two hits. Preston Ward and Carl Furillo were the only two

Dodgers to score. The Phillies demolished Brooklyn 10 to 2. Still, Dodgers fans spilled out onto the streets of Brooklyn with their heads held high. "We'll get 'em next time!" was our battle cry.

"What did you think about the game?" Dad asked as we waited for the train to come into the station.

I smiled up at my father. "Even though we lost," I began, "this was the most exciting day of my life. But . . . Dad," I continued, "I have one question."

"What is it, son?"

"How did you arrange for us to meet Jackie Robinson?"

Dad chuckled. "That was between your mother and Mrs. Robinson. They made all the arrangements. You're a lucky boy, Steve."

"I am lucky, Dad," I replied.

The next day was Saturday, so I wandered over to the Robinsons' house to thank Mrs. Robinson.

"Good afternoon, Steve," she said, opening the front door. "Please come in. Jackie Junior will be so happy to see you."

I stepped into the living room, where little Jackie was on the carpet playing with a set of wooden blocks. "Thank you for setting up the meeting between me and Mr. Robinson."

"I hope you thanked your mother, Steve. She had more to do with that meeting than I did."

"How come?"

"I ran into your mother early in the week and she told me you were very disappointed that you hadn't met Jack." Mrs. Robinson paused. "I guess he's Jackie to you, right?"

"He told me that it would be all right if I called him Jackie instead of Mr. Robinson," I explained.

"Perfectly all right, Steve. And you can call me Rachel, too. Anyway, your mom told me that you were upset because you hadn't met Jack. We decided to do something about that. It was simple, really. Jack was happy to meet you," Rachel said.

"But I didn't say anything to him," I protested.

"That was part of your charm, Steve. He knows that you'll get more comfortable being around him. At home, Jack's a husband and father. He'll be easier for you to relate to."

"That's what my mom says, too."

"Want to stay and play with little Jackie?"

"Sure do," I replied.

It was well into summertime, when everyone in the neighborhood basically lived out of doors. One evening I was outside playing stoopball by myself when the Robinsons came out on their stoop.

"Hey, Steve," Jackie yelled over to me.

I waved and went back to hitting the Spalding against the corners of our steps. I hardly noticed Jackie walk over to get a closer look.

"What game is that?" he asked me.

"We call it stoopball," I replied.

"Can I see the ball?"

I handed Jackie the rubber ball. He squeezed it several times, then handed it back to me.

"Wanna try?" I suggested.

"You bet," Jackie replied.

"You've got to hit the ball against the corners of the step and catch it before it bounces. Like this," I said, then demonstrated the perfect hit.

Jackie and I battled it out for over an hour. He was a natural. I also found out how competitive he was! Luckily, we didn't keep score. I was finally starting to feel comfortable around him!

As the season progressed, a friendship between our two families grew. Sometimes I'd visit the

Robinsons alone. Other times Mom came with me. A couple of times the Robinsons came to our house for dinner.

The shyness I initially felt around Jackie passed. One night, over steak and baked potatoes, Jackie brought up fan mail.

"Quite honestly, I'm overwhelmed by all the fan mail," he told us. "I just don't have the time to answer each and every fan."

"Jack, I think I can help," my mother offered.

"Sarah, are you sure?" Rachel cut in.

"Absolutely, I'd love it," Mom said.

"Archie, do you have any objections?" Jackie asked.

"It's fine with me," my father replied.

I sat back, listening to the adults talk, thinking this was too cool. Maybe I'd also get to read fan mail for Jackie. What a treat!

The Hero Two Doors Down

Some evenings after a hard Dodgers game, I'd wait on my stoop, hoping to chat with Jackie when he got home from Ebbets Field. I kept up with all of the team's batting averages and stolen bases so we'd have something specific to talk about.

One afternoon I was at the Robinsons' house building blocks with Jackie Junior when Jackie showed up. I watched as he bent down and scooped his son into his arms. Little Jackie squealed with delight. I couldn't take my eyes off the two. As Jackie set his son down, I very nearly expected to be picked up next. I smiled up at Jackie as he patted me on my head. "Hello, Steve. What have you and Jackie been playing today?"

I looked down at the half-built house, then back up at Jackie. "A house in the country," I told him. "We're going to make a barn, too, so the animals will have a place to live."

Jackie chuckled. "Funny, that's my dream. Well, maybe not the animal part, but I'd like a house with enough land so Jackie could have a dog."

When Rachel walked out of the kitchen, Jackie hugged her and asked, "What smells so good? I'm starving."

Rachel chuckled. "I'm making a roast and baked potatoes."

"Steve, can you stay for dinner?" Jackie asked.

"I have to ask my mother," I said, following Rachel into the kitchen.

"Call your mother, Steve. I'd be happy to talk with her," Rachel offered.

As soon as Mom gave the okay, Jackie and I cleaned up the building blocks and chased each other around the house, playing tag until dinner.

"Rachel tells me that you have a birthday coming up," Jackie said to me after he'd blessed the food and served our plates.

"I'll turn nine on June nineteenth," I replied.

"Nine," Jackie repeated. "You're in third grade. How are your grades?"

"Pretty good," I replied. "I even got satisfactory grades for my behavior! Did you ever get into trouble when you were my age?"

Jackie laughed. "When I was your age, I joined a gang. We called ourselves the Pepper Street Gang. We didn't do anything really bad . . . stole some golf balls and sold them back to the golfers . . . took fruit from the stands. We got lucky. A young minister came into our lives and helped turn me around. I got out of the gang. Reverend Downs stayed on me through my army days. Later, he married Rachel and me. I loved that guy and didn't want to disappoint him. I never knew my father, Steve. Reverend Downs died recently. I was crushed. He was still a young man. That news hurt me deeply, as if I'd lost my best friend . . . I'm sure that has something to do with my not playing my best at the start of the season."

"That's a sad story," I told Jackie. "I'm lucky to have my father around. I don't want to disappoint him, either."

"You are lucky, Steve," Rachel added. "Reverend Downs was a major force in Jack's life, but Jack's always had a great deal of self-control. Even when you're an adult, there are times when you need willpower."

"What's self-control?" I asked.

"It's the ability to stop yourself from doing the things that might not be good for you," Rachel said. "Like staying cool and controlling your impulses and feelings."

"Oh, I get it. Like when I get mad now, I try not to hit someone or say mean things to them. Sometimes I ride my bike really fast up and down Tilden Avenue. It usually works, but not always."

"That's right, Steve. Sometimes you've just got to stop and remind yourself that there's another way. I take a deep breath. Let the anger settle. It's best not to act out of anger," Jackie suggested.

"You're lucky, too, Jackie. When you get mad you can steal a base or hit a homer," I added.

"I haven't hit a homer in a while, Steve," Jackie replied with a chuckle.

"You will soon, right?"

"Soon, Steve. I'm less uptight. More focused. It's bound to pay off," Jackie assured me.

"That's good to hear," I said.

"Speaking of baseball, I have a gift for you," Jackie said, passing a baseball mitt to me. "It's more for show then actual use, but I thought you'd like to have this."

I slid my stubby fingers into the leather glove. It was much too big for me. I looked up at Jackie with questioning eyes.

"It's my practice mitt," Jackie explained.

"Gee, thanks, Jackie. My friends won't believe it when I tell them where I got this glove." I was beaming and pushing hard trying to gain an inch or so into the glove.

"Enjoy it, Steve," Jackie said.

"Is this really one of the gloves you've used in the big leagues?"

"I sure did. I used it during spring training and during warm-ups before games," Jackie told me.

"It's the best present I ever got," I pronounced.

Jackie smiled. "I'm glad you like it."

The conversation changed to the news. I ate quietly while Jackie and Rachel talked about President Truman's integrating the armed forces.

"I think it will happen sometime this summer," Jackie told Rachel.

"Not if the Southerners in Congress have their way," Rachel replied.

"President Truman is considering using an executive order to push through the integration of the armed forces," Jackie explained.

"That would end discrimination in the armed services. Your success in baseball should give Truman encouragement to do whatever he has to in order to desegregate the military," Rachel replied.

"I know that dis . . . word," I announced, stumbling on the correct pronunciation for *discrimination*. "It happened to my grandparents in Russia because they were Jewish. They left Russia and came to America so they could be treated better."

"Discrimination is something that Jews and blacks have in common," Jackie said.

"You said you served in the army?" I asked.

"Sure did," Jackie replied. "I was a second lieutenant. I was stationed in Fort Hood, Texas, where the law kept black and white people separated in schools, parks, buses, and hospitals. On the army base, Negro soldiers lived in barracks separated from white soldiers. Officers couldn't even socialize together. We had different clubs.

"One day I got on a bus going from the army base into town. I had to see the doctor at the hospital. Because of the Jim Crow laws, I was supposed to move to the back of the bus to sit down. But there was a seat in the middle of the bus next to a woman I knew from the base. The bus driver and I argued, and I was arrested," Jackie explained.

"Really?" It was hard to believe that someone could get arrested just because they sat down in the wrong seat on the bus.

"Jack, you're confusing Steve. He's too young

to understand segregation and its laws," Rachel interrupted.

"I know that some of our neighbors didn't want a black family to live here," I protested. "I know that the Dodgers were the first team to have a Negro in the Majors. I know a lot 'cause my father and I talk."

Rachel smiled. "I'm sorry, Steve. You do know a lot."

"Did you go to jail?" I asked Jackie.

"No. But my case was tried in a courtroom. I knew my rights. It's a bit complicated, Steve. But because the bus was still on the army base, the laws that required black people to go to the back of the bus didn't apply. I didn't do anything wrong. I won the case and was honorably discharged from the army. So this news that soon President Truman and Congress will end discrimination in all branches of the armed services means a great deal to me and to all Americans," Jackie explained. "Do you understand, Steve?"

"Kind of," I said. "When every Major League Baseball team has black players, it will be like the armed services. Right?"

"It will be a start, Steve."

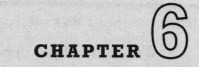

The very next day, I got into my first fistfight.

It was a warm June afternoon. The Dodgers had an off day but were starting a seven-day home stretch. After school, Sena and I rode our bikes to the school yard. I brought my new mitt along in case there was a game going on. When we arrived, kids were just taking to the field for a game of softball.

"Hey, can we play?" Sena yelled as we ran over to join them.

Sena and I were half the size of most of the kids, but we were eager to play. Sena was a better hitter than me, but I was pretty good at fielding.

"We could use you in right field," one of the boys told us.

I hated the outfield, so I started to argue, though I held my feelings back because of my talk with Jackie about self-control. The outfield reminded me of pictures I'd seen of small African boys left to herd goats in the middle of the Sahara Desert. I wanted to be in the infield where all the action was. Reluctantly, I grabbed my glove off the handlebars and ran to my position in right field.

It took several long innings before we saw any action beyond second base. Boredom had set in. I considered sitting down on the grass in protest when the next batter slammed the ball high and long. I perked up. The ball was heading toward right field. It was coming straight at me! It was my time to shine. To prove to these fourth and fifth graders that I was as good as them.

I got into position, planted my feet firmly for the catch, and looked up at my gloved hand. The glove was way too big on me. It was intended for a grown man and for a hard ball. *Too late*, I thought. It had worked for Jackie. I reached into the air as the ball began to drop.

"You need help, Steve?" Sena yelled.

"I got it!" I called out without taking my eyes off the rapidly descending ball. My heart pumped faster and faster. Salty sweat stung my eyes. I figured the batter was touching first base and heading toward second. "You won't get far," I muttered to myself as I built confidence.

The ball was within inches of my hand when I was attacked by a bee. It stung my calf and sent shooting pains up my leg. I tumbled to the ground in agony.

The ball also thumped to the ground. Sena raced over, grabbed the ball, and threw it to the pitcher while I wiped tears off my cheeks. It was too late.

The error let two runs in.

Several boys on our team ran over to me. I thought they were coming to make sure I was all right. When the first boy yelled, "Sissy!" I flinched.

Another flung a bigger insult: "Go home to your mother."

I was roaring mad. I jumped up from the ground, forgetting the painful sting, and got in their faces.

"How dare you!" I hissed. "Get stung by a bee and let's see how brave you are!"

One of the boys laughed at me. "Stung by a bee . . . yeah, right," he spat, and bent down to pick up my cherished glove. "And take this wreck of a mitt with you," he shouted.

"Jackie Robinson gave me that mitt," I shot back.

All three boys laughed. "Liar! Jackie Robinson didn't give you anything."

"Jackie's fat," one of the boys shouted.

"Yeah! He can't even steal a base this year," another boy challenged.

Now I was really, really mad. It was okay if the boys were making fun of me, but not Jackie. "He's the best player in baseball," I shouted back at them.

Sena grabbed my arm. "Let's get out of here," she whispered to me.

I pulled my arm away and jammed it into the belly of one of my attackers instead of retreating. The boy punched me hard in the gut. I dove into the two other boys.

Sena screamed so loud she made my ears pop. My head whipped around. "Run!" she yelled.

This time I listened. Sena and I took off at top speed and didn't look back. We reached our bikes, hopped on them, and pedaled away like we were being chased by a pack of dogs. After a few minutes of heavy riding, we looked back. Nobody was after us. The game had resumed and we were forgotten.

Sena glared at me. "Are you crazy?" she yelled at me. "Don't ever start a fight you can't finish! Those boys outnumbered us by a dozen and they were twice our size. What were you thinking?"

"Well," I stammered. "They had no right talking bad about Jackie. He's lost weight and is hitting again. He'll show them. He'll show everybody," I shouted back. I raced home, leaving Sena behind me.

I left my bike at the bottom of our front stoop and folded my frustrated frame on the top step. Mom stuck her head out from behind the front door. "Glad you're home. Did you play ball?"

"Sort of," I grunted.

"Stephen, please look at me when I'm talking to you."

"Yes, Mom," I said, standing up so we could face each other. Mom looked me up and down. I hoped she couldn't see signs of war. The dirty shirt. A ripped pocket. A bruised and sad face.

"Please come inside, Stephen. A hot shower will do wonders. You'll see," Mom said.

"Just a few more minutes, okay, Ma?"

"Ten minutes, Stephen."

My mother closed the door, and I sat back down with a loud sigh. Finally, I was about to head inside when I spotted Jackie Robinson coming up the street with groceries.

"Hi, Jackie," I called out and dashed down the steps. "Can I help?"

"I've got it, Steve," Jackie replied, pushing past me and heading up his steps. He reached the top step and turned around to me. "Back in a few," he told me. "Wait on the stoop."

"You bet," I replied, and grinned for the first time all day. I settled on the steps to Jackie's house, wondering if I should tell him about the fight. He wasn't inside more than ten minutes before re-appearing with empty hands.

"Take a walk with me, Steve," Jackie suggested.

I turned and looked toward my house. My mother would be hopping mad if I left the area with-out getting her okay.

"Don't worry," Jackie said as he patted me on the back. "Rachel telephoned your mom. We have her permission. I want to see your school."

My school, I thought, horrified. *I can't face those boys again*. I swallowed the lump in my throat. Did he know? "My school's closed," I mumbled.

"Doesn't matter," Jackie said. "Let's go."

We walked slowly, without words, for the first few minutes.

"Anything on your mind?" Jackie asked me.

I covered my mouth with my hands and coughed. "Maybe," I replied.

"Want to talk about it?"

"Uh . . . There are some boys at the school yard who aren't very nice," I said.

"Tell me more," he pressed.

I stopped walking and faced Jackie. "You know, don't you?"

"Sort of," he replied. "Sena's mother called your mom, who told Rachel . . . well, you understand. But I'd like to hear the story from you," Jackie said.

"Got into a fight," I admitted. Then I gave Jackie the blow-by-blow.

"You're not a sissy, Steve," Jackie said flat out. "But there are better ways to fight back, especially when you're outnumbered and much younger. Can you think of a better way to handle a verbal attack?"

"I'm not strong like you, Jackie," I protested.

"Yes, you are, Steve. Every situation is different, but in general, punching someone who has verbally attacked you will only make things worse. The bee sting was unfortunate and bad timing, but it wasn't your fault. Your attackers were looking for a fight. If you can, take the high road next time. You missed the ball. It happens. You strike out. The important thing is to get back up and do your best. And as for the glove," Jackie chuckled. "That was my mistake to give you a mitt intended for a man twice your size. Sorry about that. I meant for you to keep it safely in your room. Maybe show it to your friends, but it's not for you to play with now. Besides, it's meant for baseball, not softball."

I laughed so hard that all the tension left my body. "You're right about that!" I said. "But, Jackie, those boys had no right talking bad about you."

"I can handle it, Steve. Please don't try to defend me. I've heard a lot worse. Besides, I did come back to work overweight. It's up to me to get back to my playing shape. I'm almost there," Jackie said. "So should we pay those boys a visit?"

"You mean go over to the school yard?" I asked.

"That's right," Jackie replied.

"Wow! You mean you and me?"

Our slow walk up Tilden Avenue was interrupted every couple of feet by autograph seekers. Jackie was patient and polite to all the kids. I stood four feet two inches, but I grew taller with each step. By the time we reached school, I felt ten feet tall.

The softball game was breaking up as we approached the field. The kids who'd been mean to me an hour ago now stood silently. When the shock wore off, they flocked around Jackie.

I stepped back, but Jackie grabbed my arm and pulled me to his side. We were a pair. I beamed up at him. We were friends. As the realization sank in, I relaxed. *That's it!* I thought. *Jackie Robinson has become my friend.*

Jackie's face eased into his signature broad, warm smile. "I was hanging out with my friend Steve, and he suggested that I come by and meet you all," Jackie told the kids.

"Really?" one of the boys asked.

"We didn't mean to chase Steve away," another said, and several chimed in.

"You don't look fat, Jackie," a chubby boy suggested.

"Shut up," one of the big boys warned.

"No need for that," Jackie chastised the boy. "He's right. For the first half of the season, I was overweight. It affected my playing. I'm known for my speed on the base path and for stealing bases. It's hard to be daring and fast when you're out of shape. My weight's almost back where I need to be."

"Gee, Steve, thanks for bringing Jackie to meet us," one of the girls said. "We always hear you talking about Jackie Robinson, but nobody believed you really knew him."

"Yeah. We just thought you were lying," another boy said.

All I could do was smile.

"Will you sign my cap, Jackie?" someone asked.

"Gotta pen?"

Within seconds, boys and girls were lined up to have something signed by Jackie. A couple of kids even had me sign *my* name. I couldn't believe how proud I felt.

"I don't get to play much softball," Jackie told

the kids after he'd finished signing. "But I'd be happy to show you some skills that don't involve a ball."

The requests came in as if they were fast pitches. And Jackie fielded them like the pro he was.

"Can you teach us how to steal a base?" one of the girls asked.

"My name's Sam," a boy said, stepping forward to shake Jackie's hand. "I'm pigeon-toed, too. I want to be able to run as fast as you."

"Sam, if you really want to run faster, join the track team and work hard. You'll be fine."

"Could you show us how to slide into a base and not get caught?" another asked.

"I'll show you some moves," Jackie promised. "But keep in mind that stealing bases takes daring and patience at the same time. You must study the pitcher and run at the right moment. There's risk, for sure. If you get picked off, let it go and don't be afraid to try again."

"Hey, Jackie," one kid yelled. "I know you're from Pasadena. So will you go home after the season?"

"Not sure," Jackie replied. "California will always be home, but I think it's time to set down some roots on the East Coast. Now, enough talk. Let's play ball."

Jackie joined us on the field and took us through base-running techniques until we could all slide into home plate like him. It was so much fun. Everyone groaned when Jackie called time-out.

"Game day tomorrow," Jackie said.

"Who are you playing?" someone asked.

"Cincinnati Reds," Jackie told them.

"Good luck beating the Reds," the kids shouted as we made our way back down Tilden Avenue.

"Steve, how'd you like to invite your entire class to a Dodgers game?"

"Would I ever! My birthday's on the nineteenth," I reminded Jackie.

"Great! How about you celebrate your birthday with your class on June twenty-fourth? Right before school lets out for the summer, the Dodgers have a doubleheader against Pittsburgh. I'll get a batch of tickets to the first game. It's in the afternoon. How many kids are in your class?"

"Maybe twenty-five," I replied. "Is that too many tickets?"

"I'll get enough so parents and teachers can come. Do you think Miss Maliken will come along?"

"Are you kidding? She's a huge fan."

"You can ride over early with Rachel, Jackie, and me. We'll leave the tickets at will-call. I'll have the Dodgers office contact Miss Maliken to make all the arrangements, and ask Rachel to call your mother. And, Steve . . . you can either stay with Rachel or join your classmates for the game. Okay?"

I couldn't believe my ears! "Okay," I repeated. "It's the best news ever!"

CHAPTER 7

I was the school hero. News quickly spread that I'd brought Jackie Robinson to the school yard and he'd met a bunch of fourth and fifth graders. After the Dodgers front office called Miss Maliken, my whole third-grade class hugged me. Miss Maliken even pulled me aside and told me how happy she was with the change in my behavior. I was not the same boy who'd pushed her into that bush earlier in the year. That was because of Jackie.

I felt sorry for Sena. She was in a different third-grade class and felt left out. "How come you didn't get my class tickets, too?" she pouted on our way home from school.

"Gee whiz, Sena! I didn't forget you. Miss Maliken saved you two tickets so your mother can come with you."

"Yippee!" Sena shouted right there in the hallway leading to our classrooms.

"When the game starts, I can sit with Mrs. Robinson or with my class."

"If I were you, I'd stay with Mrs. Robinson," Sena suggested. "Her seats will be better."

The morning of June 24, I was up early. Mom and I walked over to the Robinsons' home and found Jackie Senior playing stoopball with little Jackie.

"Good morning," Jackie called out as we approached.

"Good morning," Mom and I said in unison. I continued to play stoopball with little Jackie while Jackie Senior and my mom talked out plans for the day.

"Are you excited?" Rachel asked after she came outside and Mom headed back home.

"Couldn't even sleep!" I answered, lifting Jackie Junior into the air.

"Evie." Jackie Junior giggled as I swung him around and around until my arms ached. "Down," he said.

I set little Jackie down. "Did you hear that the subway fare is going up to a dime on July first?" I asked.

"I heard," Jackie replied. "But we're not taking the subway today."

"We're not?"

"It's a special day," Jackie replied. "We're taking

a cab to Ebbets Field," Jackie Senior told Rachel. "Steve, hold Jackie's hand while I grab us a cab."

A few minutes later, we piled into the backseat. Mr. Robinson pulled his son onto his lap. I sat between Rachel and Jackie as though I was a member of their family.

We reached the player entrance and hopped out of the car.

"Once we're on the field, I'll send for you," Jackie said as he leaned in for a kiss from Rachel. "Steve, we'll get you down to the dugout before the game starts. I'll get a ball so you can get a few autographs. Sound good?" Jackie asked.

"You bet." I was smiling so much my cheeks ached.

Jackie smiled back at me. "Shouldn't be a problem," he replied, lifting Jackie Junior up so he could give him a kiss. "Wish Daddy luck." Little Jackie leaned over and planted a kiss on his dad's cheek. "That's my boy."

Jackie rushed off to the clubhouse to change into his uniform. And Rachel hurried us through the turnstile and into the belly of the ballpark. Our seats were several rows up from the Dodgers dugout. I could hear the players joking around with one another.

I couldn't stay in my seat. Luckily, neither could Jackie Junior. It was so early that the stadium was practically empty. Jackie Junior and I stood in our row and tossed a ball to each other. A couple of times the ball got away from us. Little Jackie clapped and jumped up and down.

"Enough," Rachel scolded the third time it happened.

Jackie cried out in protest until his mom hoisted him onto her knees and pointed to his father on the field.

The Dodgers were wrapping up their batting practice when we were escorted down to the Dodgers dugout. The players stopped by to greet Rachel and tickle Jackie Junior while I collected autographs from Arky Vaughan, Preacher Roe, and Gil Hodges.

"Gee, thanks" was all I could think of to say.

While the Pittsburgh Pirates took batting practice, Rachel got us hot dogs and orange juice. We brought bags of peanuts back to our seats in time for the start of the first game. I yelled from the moment the Brooklyn Dodgers took to the field. In the bottom of the first inning, Jackie hit a line drive into the right field, stole third base, and scored.

Rachel turned to me and said, "You and your class are bringing Jack good luck!"

"I hope so," I said, beaming.

Jackie's great performance continued. The fifth inning had us on our feet from start to finish! Dick

Whitman got on base with a walk. Jackie hit a ground ball to left field, and Vaughan scored!

Little Jackie and I jumped up.

"Sit down, boys," Rachel told us as Carl Furillo stepped into the batter's box. We watched quietly as Furillo grounded out. We were back on our feet when Pee Wee warmed up.

"Pee Wee! Pee Wee!" we shouted. Pee Wee's fly ball sent Jackie to third base.

A wild pitch by Elmer Riddle gave Jackie the opening he needed. With expert timing and speed, Jackie stole home.

The fans were on their feet, screaming with joy. It was so loud in the stadium that Jackie Junior covered his ears. Rachel lifted him in her arms.

"He did it, Jackie," she told her son. "You and Steve brought Daddy luck."

The Dodgers beat the Pirates 6 to 2.

My whole class and Miss Maliken wrote a letter to Jackie and Rachel to thank them for the tickets. Miss Maliken said she could see the positive influence spending time with Jackie had had on me.

The baseball game was the best birthday present I could have asked for. But my parents had also gotten me an incredible gift. They had given it to me on my birthday, a few days before the game. It was wrapped in bright silver paper. I tore into it and revealed a Cleveland model kit for the L-17 airplane. I couldn't believe it!

On Sunday, June 27, Dad and I went down into the basement to work on our model airplane. "Steve, this L-17 model is a major step up from the kids' model airplane kits you're used to," Dad began. "I've watched you closely and feel that your building skills merit this upgrade."

"Awesome," I said, studying the photo of a sleek

chrome plane on the front of the box. It cost a dollar instead of ten cents like my other models. "How come this kit cost so much?"

"This model is more complicated to build. We can add a fuel tank and landing gears. It won't fly, but this is the real deal. We'll have to work on this one together. It will take time and lots of patience. Are you up for that?"

"You bet," I replied. I was used to making model planes all by myself in an afternoon. "How much time do you think it will take?" I asked.

"Most of the summer," Dad replied.

"Jeez . . . that is a long time."

Dad and I began to work that same night. We studied the plans and mapped out a strategy to build our plane.

"They used this type of aircraft during World War Two. It was built for reconnaissance, and to carry both soldiers and light cargo. Our model will look just like the real thing except it'll be made out of balsa wood." Dad looked up at the framed cover of a *Saturday Evening Post* that hung on the wall over our workbench. It was dated December 9, 1944. The cover picture showed a boy building a model plane, with the headline ALL BOYS WERE EXPECTED TO MAKE MODEL AIRPLANES.

"Let's start building the basic plane by cutting out the parts printed on this large piece of wood. I'll cut out the pieces, and you can sand the edges until they're smooth and the exact shape of their outline. As soon as you were born, I dreamed of this moment," Dad said.

"What moment?" I asked.

"The moment when you and I would build our first model plane," Dad explained.

"Why was it so important?"

"I grew up loving baseball and building model airplanes and couldn't wait to share those two favorite things with you. It's a dream come true, son."

Tears came to my eyes. We quit talking and finished sanding the last pieces of wood.

Dad and I worked together on the plane most Sundays. We'd spend hours cutting and sanding pieces. We'd stop briefly for lunch, then get back to work until Mom called us for dinner. Some evenings I worked alone.

A month into our summer project, the wings and tail were complete and we'd begun to work on the fuselage. The body of the plane was the most complicated because of the curves. It took two more weeks to finish fitting small pieces of balsa to the open rectangles that formed the body of the plane.

One hot afternoon I came home from stickball and headed straight for the basement. My father was down there bent over our model airplane.

"Hey, Dad," I called from the staircase.

"Hi, Steve," he replied.

I knew immediately that something was wrong. "How come you didn't wait for me?"

Dad looked up. His eyes were red. "Sorry, Steve. There was some bad news today, so I came down here as soon as I got home and started working," he replied.

I stepped in closer. "What happened?"

"Babe Ruth died today of cancer," Dad said.

"Gee, Dad, that's terrible."

"His body will lie in state at the main entrance to Yankee Stadium for two days. I'm going over there tomorrow."

"Can I go with you?"

"It's going to be very crowded with long lines. Besides, you have school." Dad paused.

"Did you ever get to see him play?" I asked.

"It was a little before my time," Dad replied.

"The Babe was a baseball legend. Did you know he hit 714 home runs in his career? He was a real New York character. Everyone loved him . . . even Dodgers fans. We'll remember August sixteenth as the date we lost one of MLB's greatest," Dad said, blowing his nose into his handkerchief. "Come on, son. Let's see if we can finish up this fuselage today. I know it's tedious work, but we're getting close."

"Sure, Dad," I agreed, climbing onto a stool next to my father. I knew he was upset, but I hoped that working on this with me would make him feel a little bit better.

We worked in silence. When the fuselage was finished, we sanded the model plane and covered it with layers of tissue paper and fabric, then final thin strips of balsa wood. Before going to bed, we painted our plane chrome and finished it off with a red stripe down the middle. It was a beauty!

The next Sunday, Dad took me to the field where people were showing off their model planes. We set ours up on a folding table and waited for someone to notice it. Dad circled around the other tables and I manned ours.

"That's an L-17, isn't it, boy?" an older man said as he approached our table.

"Sure is," I replied with pride.

"The finish is nice and smooth. It looks like it could fly," the man said.

"My dad and I still have some work to do. We don't even have landing gear," I told him.

"I was an air force pilot during the Second World War. I delivered cargo to North Africa in one of these babies." The man ran his fingers over the fuselage. "You did a good job."

"That's because I made it with my father," I replied.

"That's right," the man said. "Stick around. Some of the boys will be flying their models this afternoon. For such a young boy, you're taking this hobby seriously. I like that," he added.

By the time Dad came back to the table, I was beaming. "Dad! Tons of people came by to admire our plane."

"I'm proud of you, son."

"Can we build one that flies?" I asked.

"Sure."

It wasn't as if we forgot about the Dodgers that summer. Building the model plane just gave us something to do with our hands while we listened to games on the radio. It also kept us from being too anxious when the Dodgers went from last place to third in late August.

The Dodgers left Brooklyn for a long stretch of away games. I overheard Rachel tell my mom that when Jackie was playing out of town, he wrote her long letters and sent flowers on Fridays. Mom said that her husband needed to take some romance lessons from Jackie. The two mothers laughed a long time over that one.

I told my father about the conversation between Mom and Rachel. Dad reminded me that since he worked in Manhattan, he didn't need to write his wife love letters. I had to agree. My father worked long hours, but he came home every night. I counted myself lucky.

On August 29, Jackie "hit for the cycle" with a home run, a triple, a double, and then a single in the same game! Jackie also stole a base, scored three runs, and knocked in two others. Seven wins in a row sent the Dodgers into first place. Boy, did we celebrate that night!

The new school year started up after Labor Day. A new class and a new teacher!

After a few tough breaks, the Dodgers ended

their season in third place. We were heartbroken about their missing the playoffs. I refused to cry, but it took me a whole day before I could even talk about how sad I felt.

Sena and I were on our way home from school. We'd been fourth graders for a whole month. As we turned onto our block, I spotted Jackie.

"Hi, Steve," Jackie said as we walked toward him. "Is this your friend Sena?"

"Sure is."

"Nice to finally meet you, Sena," Jackie said, extending his right hand to her. "Steve talks about you all the time."

"He talks to me about you, too, Mr. Robinson. You're his hero," Sena said.

"I'm his friend, Sena," Jackie replied, rubbing my shoulder. "How's fourth grade?" he asked.

"Pretty tough. A lot more homework," we told him.

"Do you see much of Miss Maliken?"

"I pass her in the hall every day," I replied. "She asked if you were still my neighbor. She told me to keep up the good work."

"Sena, did you have trouble with Miss Maliken last year, too?" Jackie asked.

"You bet," Sena replied. "She had a right to be tough on us."

"From the stories Steve told me, I guess you're correct."

"Were you okay with the Dodgers' record this season?" Sena asked.

"My only disappointment was that we ended up in third place. We could have done better."

"But you led the league in hits, doubles, triples, total bases, and runs scored. Plus, you were rated the best second baseman in the National League. You've got to be happy with those statistics," I reminded Jackie.

"Baseball's a team sport," Jackie replied. "No individual player can rest on his performance alone. Our team had a chance to be first and we blew it."

"What's next for you?" Sena asked.

Jackie rested his hands on his hips and stared down at Sena and me. "One thing for sure," he said, "I won't be eating as much as I did the last winter break."

Sena and I cracked up.

"Are you and Rachel going to California to see your families?"

"Not this year, Steve. We're staying in New York. Campy and I are going barnstorming for a month. We'll be playing with a Negro League team, the New York Cubans. But we'll be back in New York by November to work at the Harlem YMCA."

"Phew," I said, relieved. "I thought you'd be away for months."

Jackie smiled down at me. "As a matter of fact, Rachel and I have decided to plant some roots here in New York."

"What does that mean?" I asked, feeling happy and hopeful that the Robinsons would remain my neighbors.

"We're house hunting. It's time we bought a house with a yard so Jackie can play outside."

"You mean you're moving off Tilden Avenue?" I asked.

"At some point," Jackie replied. I couldn't believe it. Jackie and I had just become friends and now there was a chance he might move away? I was crushed, but I didn't want Jackie to see that. Sena and I said good-bye and I went home.

The next day, I was sent to the principal's office because I bloodied a classmate's nose. I hadn't been in trouble since last spring. I could tell right away that Mrs. Wexler was very disappointed in me.

"What do you have to say for yourself?" she asked me.

"Joel deserved it," I muttered, still angry about the fight.

"Stephen, no one deserves to get punched in the face," she told me. "Did you two argue about something?"

"Joel told me, 'I'll bust your chops.' So I beat him to it," I said defiantly. "Last week, he called me a chicken just because I said it was too cold to play football."

"Still no reason to hit another person, Stephen," Mrs. Wexler reminded me. "Your mother wasn't home, so I've called your father. He's on his way to the office to get you."

"Oh, no," I said. "You made my father leave work to come and get me?"

"That's correct," Mrs. Wexler said. "This is a serious offense. A parent has to be notified. While you're waiting for your father, you can write a letter of apology to Joel."

"Does Joel have to write me an apology letter, too?"

"I'm meeting with Joel after lunch," Mrs. Wexler replied.

An hour later, Dad marched into the office and snatched me up from my chair. "We'll talk about your behavior at home," he growled.

The walk home was brisk and silent. I could tell my father was furious with me and especially for being called out of work.

"I thought you'd learned not to overreact, Steve," he yelled at me as soon as we stepped inside the house.

"Don't I have the right to defend myself?"

"Not with your fists, Stephen."

"You mean I wouldn't have gotten into trouble if I'd called Joel a fathead or sissy?"

"Don't talk back to me," Dad shouted. "School is a place for study, not fighting of any kind. You are to be respectful to your teachers and your class-mates. Do you understand me?"

"What do I say if one of them disrespects me?"

"Tell your teacher and let her handle the situation."

"And have the whole class laughing at me? No way!" I said.

"Then be prepared to spend the entire fourth grade on punishment. No stickball. No building model airplanes. No sledding. Is that what you want?"

I shook my head. "No," I said quietly. "Dad, I'm one of the shortest kids in my class. I've got to stand up for myself. Just got to," I said, sinking down to the floor in frustration.

Dad pulled up a chair beside me. "What's got-ten into you? Your mother and I haven't had any trouble from you in a long time. Are you angry about something?"

I started to cry. "Jackie's moving off Tilden Avenue. I won't ever see him again," I said between sobs. Jackie was already away barnstorming, and I wouldn't see him for weeks. I couldn't imagine what it would be like when he was gone for good.

"Come here, son," Dad said, pulling my arm so I'd stand up. "Dry up your tears. You've made a special friendship with the Robinsons. They don't have to live next door for you to continue being friends. We'll help you stay in touch."

"You mean I can see the Robinsons even when they move away?"

"That's right," Dad said. "Plus, we'll go to Ebbets Field when the Dodgers are in town. You can write letters to the Robinsons. And I'll bet you can even visit." Dad paused. "It won't be the same as having them as neighbors, but you'll always be friends. As you get older, son, you'll make lots more friends. That's the way it works."

"I hope so," I said, reaching over to hug my father.

"Promise me you'll settle back down at school. That's your job now. You can't afford to be pulled out of class for misbehaving, and I certainly can't afford to miss work. Is that clear?"

"Yes, Dad," I replied. "I'll finish my letter to Joel now. I'm going to tell him that name-calling doesn't solve a problem. Maybe we can start being friends."

A month later, I was outside playing football with some of the kids in the neighborhood when Jackie returned home from barnstorming. It was a warm, early November afternoon. My friends and I had taken over the block for our game.

"Jackie!" I yelled as he stepped out of the cab.

Jackie dropped his bags on the stoop and walked over to us.

"Hey, Steve!" he said to me, then greeted the others.

"Glad you're back," I said.

"Me too," Jackie replied.

"Throw me a pass, Jackie," I pleaded.

"Just one, Steve," he agreed.

I handed him the football, then turned to run down the street. When I'd reached a nice distance, I turned back around and skipped backward, waiting for Jackie to release the football. I lifted my arms to catch the ball, suddenly realizing that this was a ball spiraling in my direction, thrown by a professional athlete who'd played semipro football with the Honolulu Bears! Yikes!

My heart pounded. My knees buckled. My hands began to sting, and the ball hadn't even reached them yet. Was I crazy?

The ball came in so hard against my chest that it literally knocked me over.

I hit the ground with a thump.

The ball was still cradled between my hands and my chest. I lifted the ball high above my head and let out a roar!

CHAPTER 8

On Sunday, December 19, we were walloped by a snowstorm that lasted twenty hours, leaving behind almost twenty inches of snow and record cold temperatures. I watched the whole thing from the windows of our house, counting down the hours before Sena and I could go sledding.

While I was dreaming of snowball fights and racing down the big hill in the park, my mother was making plans for our big Hanukkah gathering. This year, Hanukkah would begin on December 26. The first night was a big deal. Our house would be filled with grandparents, uncles, aunts, and cousins. I loved everything about Hanukkah except getting dressed up for dinner and being beaten in the dreidel game by my older cousins. Mom would make the potato pancakes, applesauce, and sugary donuts first thing in the morning; set out the bowl of wooden dreidels and foil-wrapped chocolate Hanukkah gelt; then place the menorah and candies on the dining room table just before company arrived.

Naturally, the very thought of getting eight gifts made me giddy. Mom pretty much knew what I wanted, but I made a list and gave it to her when I came down for breakfast.

"Can I go sledding today?" I asked as soon as I walked into the kitchen.

"Please eat your breakfast, and then we'll discuss plans for the day," my mother said.

"Okay," I replied.

"How about scrambled eggs with your bagel?"

"No, thank you."

My mother was standing next to the counter with a wet cloth in her right hand and our menorah in front of her.

"Did you sleep well?" Mom asked.

"Yep," I replied, settling into my chair and slapping jelly on my bagel.

Mom looked at me as though she had something important to say. "Steve, you know that there is a war in Israel," Mom began.

I nodded. The Arab-Israeli War had been a dinner table conversation for months. I didn't *really* understand war. How did they get started? Who was right? Who was wrong? Was the fight for freedom or land? Did children still go to school? Since I'd never experienced a war, it was strange to me.

"Maybe we could bring all the children in Israel to America so they'll be safe," I suggested.

Mom dropped the cloth she'd been using to clean our menorah and walked around the kitchen counter to take a seat at the table. "Steve, you're the kindest boy," she said. "I can just imagine millions of Jewish and Arab children coming to America so they can go to school, be loved, and live in a safe place. Unfortunately, that is not possible. But we can help make a difference in their lives."

"Really? How?" I asked, happy to know there was a solution.

"Your father and I have talked about this a lot and we have a suggestion. Next Sunday we'll celebrate the first night of Hanukkah. The family will come to our house and we'll begin our holiday. Your father and I would like to make this first night of

Hanukkah have a special meaning beyond a family gathering and the exchange of gifts. We want it to truly be about our Jewish faith. You know how we talk about 'doing a mitzvah'?"

"Sure," I said. "It's doing a good deed, like when we visit the home for old people and plant flowers in their garden."

"That's right, Steve. On Sunday when your father lights the first candle, he will say a special prayer asking for peace in Israel and then tell our family of our plan to send money to help support both Arab and Jewish children in Israel," Mom said.

"But the children are so far away. How will we get money to them?"

"We will send money to them through the United Nations organization called UNICEF. It helps children all around the world. Since the Arab-Israeli War began, UNICEF has been providing food and supplies to Palestinians who had to flee from their homes, and to Israeli women and children who are caught in the middle of a war. We will ask your grandparents, aunts, uncles, and even you and your cousins to give us money to send to UNICEF."

"I only have two dollars," I said.

Mom chuckled. "We have another idea of how you and your cousins can contribute."

"You do?"

"Yes, we want you to give up one of your Hanukkah gifts," Mom said.

"You're going to send toys to the kids in Israel?" I asked.

"No. They need food and blankets more than toys. Instead of buying you eight gifts, we'll buy you seven smaller gifts. The money that we save will be added to money your father and I have put aside to send to Israel. Your aunts and uncles are asking your cousins to make the same small sacrifice. You and your cousins will be doing a mitzvah."

I wrestled with Mom's words for a few minutes. I put my bagel down and sat back in my chair. It made sense, but I was a little disappointed. "Where do children go to get away from bombs?" I asked.

"Sometimes, they hide with their families in shelters dug underground. But since bombs and gunfire can happen all day or night, they sometimes hide under their desks at school or in corners of buildings. Truth is, there is no real hiding place. Kids are innocent victims of war."

"I've been trying to picture war," I said. "Where would we go if Tilden Avenue was hit by a bomb?"

"War is hard to imagine. I pray you will never have to experience it," Mom said. "We're safe here."

Up until this very moment, I hadn't felt connected to the Arab-Israeli War. Now I was. Mom was right—children were innocent victims. They didn't start wars. I felt sorry that they had to grow up afraid of death. Maybe doing a good deed would make some of the children feel less afraid. "I get it, Mom."

Mom lifted her right hand and settled it on top of mine. "I knew you'd understand, Stephen. You have the heart of a healer."

"What does that mean?" I asked.

"It means that you care about others. That's a good way to be," Mom said, planting a kiss on my cheek.

I got up from my chair and walked over to the counter where my list lay, untouched. To do a good deed, I'd have to give up something expensive from my list. I picked it up and crossed out the Diesel Road Roller, a toy I'd seen advertised in the *Brooklyn Eagle*. I knew that it was my most expensive gift.

"Thank you, Steve," Mom said as she smiled down at me. "I have one more request."

"What's that?" I asked.

"We'd like to include a letter from you to the children along with the check."

"What would I say?"

"Think about what you'd like to say if you had a friend who lived in Israel and was surrounded by war," Mom said, handing me a pad of paper. "Write what's in your heart."

"To who?"

"You could start 'Dear Friend,'" Mom suggested.

I sat back down and tried to imagine the real sounds of gunfire and bombs going off around me. My hands trembled as I began to write.

Dear friend,
My name is Stephen Satlow. I live in
Brooklyn, New York, where there is no war.
My family and I want to help, but we can't
stop the bombing. We're sending you money
so you can eat and blankets so you won't be

cold. *We will pray that peace will come soon and you can live where it is safe. You are so brave. I hope we meet someday.*

> *Sincerely,*
>
> *Steve*

CHAPTER 9

By early Monday morning, the snowstorm had finally slowed, leaving the usually bustling city stilled under mountains of white powder. Only a few cars, taxis, and buses braved the elements to crawl up newly plowed streets narrowed by rows of trapped cars.

Despite the snowstorm, school was not closed. From my bedroom window, I could see kids bursting out of apartment buildings and low-rise brick houses, intent on adventure as they walked to school.

Once class let out, the real fun began. Dressed in layers of flannel and wool, I met Sena outside my house. We set out dragging our sleds to a patch of open hilly property.

"Be careful," my mother yelled down to us from the top landing of our front stoop. "The roads are barely plowed. Cars will be slipping and sliding with drivers who think they're in control but aren't."

"We'll be fine, Mom," I yelled back.

"Keep your eyes alert to icy patches."

Sena and I proceeded up Tilden Avenue past our school and onward. For a while, we pretended not to be cold. Instead, I kept telling myself that we were on an adventure.

"I can barely feel my fingertips," Sena complained. We were just two blocks from my house.

"Put your free hand inside your coat pocket," I suggested.

"Can't," she said.

"How come?"

"Because I need both hands to pull this sled," Sena told me. "It's heavy, Steve."

I felt sorry for Sena. She was about my height but thinner. I wasn't big enough to pull two sleds. "Three more blocks, Sena. Surely you can make that?" I peeked over at her, hoping she'd rally to the challenge.

"Didn't say I changed my mind," she muttered.

Finally, we reached our destination. It was a neighborhood winter wonderland. The hills were packed with kids sledding. Laughter and screams pierced the snowy calm. Snowballs were being hurled from every direction.

Out of the corner of my eye, I caught Sena smiling and thought she was up to something. I dropped my sled and turned away from her, looking for a good spot to sled. A ball of wet, cold snow splattered against my jacket. I felt the sting against my left shoulder and turned back to Sena. Grabbing a wad of snow, I hurled it at her.

Sena stood straight in defiance, daring me to hit her again. "Game on!" we screamed at the same time.

We battled, laughing so hard we were weak from struggle. After a good twenty rounds, I quit. With soggy woolen mittens and frozen fingers, I surrendered.

Sena and I climbed up the less crowded side of the hill, hopped on our sleds, and sped down, screaming as if wolves were chasing us. This uphill/downhill play continued until we could no longer feel our fingers or toes.

I made it back home in time to see Jackie shoveling his front steps. I stopped to chat.

"Hey, Steve. Where've you been?"

"Sledding," I told him.

"At the 47th Street park?"

"No. My friend Sena and I went to an area with lots of hills. The place was packed with kids," I explained. "We had so much fun!"

"I've never gone sledding," Jackie mused. "It must be fun. I'll put that on my list for Jackie and me to do when he's older."

"Sure is cold today," I said, shivering.

"In Southern California, where I grew up, it didn't get this cold."

"Really," I responded in surprise. "What happens in winter, then?"

Jackie chuckled. "Guess California doesn't have much of a winter. Not like the East Coast, anyway. It's mostly warm year-round. If the temperature drops down to the 50s or 60s, we wear a light jacket. About this time of year, I'd be on the golf course, not shoveling snow. But since I plan to play baseball for the Brooklyn Dodgers a long time, I better get used to this cold weather."

Jackie finished clearing the last two steps. "Want to come in and have some hot chocolate?"

"I better get home now," I told him.

"Do you have family coming over this weekend?"

"A bunch."

"That'll be nice. We don't have much family here. Maybe you can come by on Thursday. We'll be decorating for the holiday and it'll be more fun for Jackie if you're there. Would you like that?"

"Would I!"

"Great, but get your parents' permission. Come over around one. We'll send you back home by three."

On Thursday, I carried my L-17 model plane with me to the Robinsons'.

Rachel opened the door and wrapped her arms around me. "Come on in quickly and warm up. Jack and Jackie Junior are in the living room, decorating our tree."

"I made this plane," I said, holding it up so Rachel could get a good view.

"Wow!" she said. "That is incredible. Is it a replica of a plane used during World War Two?"

"Sure is," I replied. "How'd you know?"

"Oh, I worked on war planes as a riveter."

"What's a riveter?" I asked.

"It was a name given to women who worked in American factories during World War Two," Rachel explained. "A rivet is a metal pin. They were hammered into the war planes to hold pieces of the plane together. It was my job to stand inside the plane while the metal bolts were hammered from the outside through holes on the inside. I'd yell to the person outside the plane to let them know that the bolt was coming through the hole. The war was far away, and women couldn't fight. We wanted to help out and it sure felt good when we did."

"That is so cool," I said.

"How's your mother, Steve?"

"She's getting ready for our big family dinner Sunday," I replied.

"I'll bet she is," Rachel said. "Go on into the living room and see if you can help my husband. Between the lights and little Jackie, he's got his hands full. I'm headed into the kitchen to make a snack. Are you hungry?"

"Not really," I replied.

"How about some hot chocolate?"

"Yes, please!"

When I walked into the living room, my mouth dropped open. Jackie was standing on a ladder next to a giant tree. I'd never ever seen a tree inside any-one's house.

"Evie!" Jackie Junior screamed when he saw me. I lifted my little friend into the air, swung him around, and set him back on the floor. He was just beginning to say words we could understand.

"Hi, Jackie," I called up.

"Glad you made it, Steve!"

I moved in closer to the evergreen tree. It smelled like the woods and nearly touched the ceiling. Jackie was stringing colored lights through its branches. He looked down and smiled. "You're just in time to help me string these lights around the tree."

I looked up and down the huge tree. "I can't reach that high," I squeaked out.

Jackie chuckled. "Me either. That's why I have this ladder. You can still help. I'll wrap the lights around the top. You can string them around the bottom."

"Got it," I said, happy to have a part in making the tree sparkle.

Together we wound the lights from top to bottom. Then we settled around the coffee table to drink hot chocolate and admire the tree.

"It's so big and pretty!" I marveled.

"Had to get the biggest one on the lot, right, son?" Jackie said proudly. "Is your tree up yet, Steve?"

"Oh, we don't have one."

"Steve," Rachel said, "I have a special project for you and little Jackie that involves colored paper, scissors, and paste. Are you two ready to make something pretty to put on the tree?"

Jackie Junior and I clapped our hands and raced to the kitchen while Jackie carefully placed colorful bulbs on the branches of the tree. An hour later, we were laughing and stringing a paper wreath around the tree. When the tree was decorated, Rachel plugged in the lights, and Jackie Junior and I screamed with joy. It was the most beautiful tree I'd ever seen.

CHAPTER 10

Sena sledded past me and yelled, "Look out!" I used my mittened hands to increase my speed and catch up to her. We crashed into each other and toppled off our sleds, laughing and rolling in the tamped-down snow. It was the next day, and we were still making the most of the huge snowfall.

"That was amazing!" Sena screamed as we righted ourselves in the snow.

"Sure was, but I've got to go home," I said.

"Yeah, me too. It'll be dark soon."

When I got home, my parents were anxiously waiting for me.

"Stephen," Mom called out as I stepped into the front hallway.

"Yes, Mom," I answered as I began slipping out of my wet coat, hat, boots, and gloves.

"Stephen, come in here immediately," my father barked.

"Coming," I yelled back, tripping over my wet clothes as I hustled to the living room. Had I stayed at the park too long? Missed a doctor's appointment? I was searching my brain, trying to come up with a reason for my dad's bad mood. "Am I in trouble?" I asked from the doorway.

"Did you ask Jackie Robinson for a Christmas tree?" Dad demanded.

I repeated his question over in my mind. *A Christmas tree.* "No. I was over at the Robinsons' helping them decorate a tree, and Jackie asked if our tree was up. I told him no," I replied. Then I spotted the evergreen tree leaning up against a wall. It wasn't quite as tall as the Robinsons', but it sure was a beauty. "Jeepers!" I yelled. "Did Jackie buy that tree for me?"

"Are you sure you didn't say that you wanted a tree, Stephen?" Dad asked again.

"No," I repeated, confused by all the fuss over a tree. I was already thinking of ways to decorate it.

"Steve, this is not a joke. That"—Dad pointed toward the beautiful evergreen—"*is* a Christmas tree. Did you ask Jackie to get one for you?"

"No, I did not," I stated clearly. "I just told him that we didn't have one."

"Did you also tell him that we're Jewish and don't celebrate Christmas?"

"No one mentioned Christmas," I said. "We just decorated a tree like this one."

"Stephen, come sit down next to me." Mom gestured toward the couch. I slid in beside her. "Do you realize that today is Christmas Eve and tomorrow is Christmas?"

"No," I said. None of my friends talked about Christmas. They only talked about Hanukkah. "Honest, Ma . . . I didn't know that when you bring a tree like that into the house it's called a Christmas tree. I've never even seen a big tree inside someone's house until yesterday. And boy, was it pretty."

"You mean at the Robinsons' house. Right, Steve?"

"Right," I replied. "We covered it with lights and shiny, colored bulbs. Rachel even helped little Jackie and me make decorations out of colored paper. I had so much fun. No one said anything about Christmas. I just thought it was so pretty," I said, fighting back tears. "Did I do something wrong?"

Mom wrapped her arms around me. "Absolutely not, son. It's just a misunderstanding. That's all. I better call Rachel and explain."

"Dad, can I keep the tree?"

"No, Steve. It wouldn't be right," Dad replied. "This is a Christmas tree. It is a symbol of a Christian holiday. Like Hanukkah, Christmas is part religious holiday and part tradition. It is also a time when families gather around symbols, like the Christmas tree, and exchange gifts. The problem is that Jews and Christians have different beliefs and separate holidays. Your mother and I respect those differences. We appreciate that the Robinsons shared part of their religious experience with you. They may not have understood Jewish traditions and the fact that we don't celebrate Christmas. That's why it's best if your mother speaks with Rachel so there won't be any further misunderstanding."

"Won't it hurt their feelings?" I asked.

"No more than it would hurt your grandparents to come into our home and see a Christmas tree," Dad explained.

"What would Bubbe say?" I pressed.

Dad chuckled. "What will your mother say, Sarah?"

"She'd say, 'Oy vey,' and maybe even faint," Mom teased.

"Right. So get rid of it before we upset our Hanukkah dinner!" Dad said.

"We can't do that," I protested.

"We most certainly can!" my father retorted.

I was torn over what was right and wrong. The tree was a gift from Jackie Robinson to me. That made it super special, like when he gave me the practice mitt. But I understood my father's concerns. Still, it was a gift given out of friendship. I didn't want anything to spoil my relationship with Jackie.

"Mom, please don't call Rachel yet," I pleaded. "I can't just give the tree back to Jackie. There has to be a way for me to keep it. There just has to be."

"Do you understand why your father and I are concerned?" Mom asked.

"Sort of," I replied. "I get that it's not like a tree in the park. I get that it means something to families who believe in Christmas like our menorah means to us. But it doesn't have to mean Christmas to us. Does it?"

My father didn't respond. He stood tall and firm on the other side of the room while Mom and I talked quietly.

"Dad . . ." I moaned, looking over at him. "It's a gift."

"Archie, Steve has a point," Mom said, and then hesitated. "We could simply tell my parents the truth. That Steve has a special friendship with our neighbors, and they gave him the tree."

"Absolutely not," Dad boomed.

"But, Dad . . ." I pleaded.

"Sarah, take care of this," Dad demanded.

The doorbell rang just when Dad seemed to make his final judgment. He left the room to answer the door, without saying another word. A few minutes later, he stepped back into the living room with the Robinsons.

My mouth flew open. *Oh, no,* I thought. *Now Dad will spoil everything.*

I avoided looking directly at Jackie.

"Hi, Steve!" Jackie said, patting my head and smiling down at me. "Do you like your tree?"

My head bobbed up and down, but I didn't speak.

"Here, Rachel and I brought over lights and ornaments," Jackie said as he handed me a box marked FRAGILE and a wooden angel. "This angel goes on the very top of the tree."

"Gee, thanks," I said, looking from Jackie to my dad, fearful of the next words between the two.

"I hope you don't mind, Archie. If you could have seen Steve's face yesterday when he saw our tree . . . well, when Steve said he didn't have one, I just thought it would be a nice thing to share. We think so highly of your boy, Archie. He's become part of our family." Jackie talked fast and meant well.

"I appreciate the sentiment," Dad finally said.

"Sarah, I hope we didn't overstep our boundaries. I told Jack that you might be buying your tree later today," Rachel said.

"Rachel, forgive us. You've been so generous with our son. He loves spending time with you, and we appreciate your friendship," Mom replied. "I was so shocked by the gesture that I didn't respond appropriately when Jackie showed up with this lovely tree. The problem is that we're Jewish and we do not celebrate Christmas."

"Oh, my," Rachel whispered, looking from my mom to Jackie.

"I'm so sorry," Jackie apologized.

"Rachel, Jack, it's okay," my mother insisted. "We know you meant well. You see . . . until you moved into the neighborhood, Steve had very limited exposure to families from other faiths. Only Jewish families lived in this neighborhood. His school friends are all Jewish. When you invited Steve to come over, I had no idea he'd be helping you decorate your Christmas tree or I would have prepared him. This weekend, we'll begin our Hanukkah celebration. It's a Jewish holiday, and this year it just happens to fall a day after Christmas."

I looked from my mother to the Robinsons, wondering how this news would affect me. I glanced over at my father and tried to read his expression, but all the adults were focused on Mom. I realized that she was the key to how both families were working through this uncomfortable moment. It also dawned on me that keeping my friendship with the Robinsons was far more important than keeping a tree.

"Jack and I are so embarrassed," Rachel offered again.

"Our sincere apologies," Jackie added. "It didn't even occur to me that you didn't celebrate Christmas. You see, we're very much like Steve. Until we moved to Tilden Avenue, Rachel and I had very little interaction with Jewish families. I'm ashamed to admit that, until now, we didn't know much about your faith, either."

I was bursting to say something, but what should I say? I didn't want to blow it, and I knew if I said the wrong thing, I'd be in big trouble. I opened my mouth to speak, but a giggle escaped.

"Gee, Dad," I began, trying to hold my laughter at bay. "It's kinda funny."

I glanced over at Mom. Her face was red as she, too, found the situation amusing.

Mom and I started to giggle at the same time. Before we knew it, even Dad and Jackie were laughing. When we all settled back down, I popped the big question.

"Dad, you taught me to accept a gift in the spirit that it's given. Right?" I asked.

"That's right, son," my father admitted.

"Then can I keep the tree?"

Jackie jumped in. "It's all right, Steve. We made a mistake. I'll take the tree home with us."

But Dad silenced Jackie with a wave of his hands. We turned our attention to my father. "We've all learned an important lesson here today," Dad began. "I realize now that I've been inflexible. Sunday night is our first night of Hanukkah. Our extended family will gather here for prayers, the lighting of the menorah, and a special meal. Later, the children will play games. This year we've decided to dedicate the first day of Hanukkah to peace. I will lead the prayer, and others can share their perspectives. It would be wonderful if you, Rachel, and little Jackie could join us."

"We'd love to," Jackie replied.

"That's great," Dad said as he and Jackie shook hands, and Rachel and Mom hugged.

"Steve," Dad said, turning to me. "You may keep the tree. Maybe the Robinsons can help us decorate it. You were right. This tree is a gift of friendship, and we will accept it as such. We've been blessed to share this year with the Robinsons. The tree solidifies that blessing. This year, this Jewish family will have both a Christmas tree and a menorah."

Sunday afternoon, we waited for the Robinsons to arrive before saying our prayers and lighting the menorah. When Jackie walked in, my bubbe was the first to greet him.

"Mr. Robinson, it's wonderful to finally meet you. Thank you for being so generous of your time with our Stevie," she said. I trailed behind my grandmother and the Robinsons as they were introduced to my extended family. I kept hoping there would be no complaints about the Christmas tree. When Bubbe finished introductions, she pulled Jackie aside and whispered something that made him smile. Knowing my bubbe, I figured it had something to do with the Christmas tree.

Dad and Mom came out of the kitchen with the last of the platters of food and saw Bubbe talking with Jackie. They put the platters down on the long dining room table and went over to welcome the Robinsons.

"We're so happy you joined us," Dad said.

"I've already introduced them to all the family," Bubbe said.

Dad kissed my grandmother and called all of the aunts, uncles, and cousins to gather around the table. "After a short prayer, we will light one of the candles in the menorah," Dad told the Robinsons. "Jackie, would you be so good as to help light the first candle?"

Jackie looked startled. "I'd be happy to," he agreed.

"Wonderful. Don't worry about a thing. Stephen will help you," Dad said.

I looked up at the two very special men in my life and nodded in agreement. It was a big honor to be chosen to help light the candles. *A sign*, I thought, *that Dad thinks I can be trusted.*

I stood up front with my father and mother facing out toward my family and the Robinsons. I figured that if I stood up on my toes, I could also see the top of the Christmas tree. Since Jackie moved in, our lives had changed in so many unbelievable ways. I turned and looked up at my tall, handsome father and felt very proud to be his son.

"We are blessed this evening to have our Christian friends join us for this annual celebration of commitment. Hanukkah is a time for families to celebrate freedom, faith, and peace. I'd be honored if Jackie would join me in the lighting of the menorah."

After Jackie came to the front, Dad lifted me into his arms so I could reach the menorah. "Steve, please help Jackie light the shamus."

Secure in my dad's arms, I leaned over and lifted

the shamus from the center of the menorah and handed it to Jackie. My dad put me beside Jackie, who lit the shamus and then used it to light the first candle while Dad repeated a series of prayers in English.

As Dad finished speaking, my grandfather stepped forward to repeat the prayers in Hebrew. My bubbe cried softly and Dad slipped his hand in mine.

While everyone gathered in small groups to eat and talk, I sat beside Jackie and wondered how to say good-bye to him.

"Are you looking forward to the next baseball season?" I asked.

"Very much, Steve," Jackie replied. "I have a feeling 1949 will be our best season ever!"

"How come?"

"We've come a long way as a team and as a league. I no longer have to prove that I can succeed in the Major Leagues. Now we can concentrate on making it back up to first place," Jackie said.

"And you'll be living in your own house, right?"

"I hope so," Jackie said, looking directly at me. "We've got to find the right house first. Wherever we are, you'll be welcome. You know that, don't you, Steve?"

"I just needed to hear you say it," I replied.

EPILOGUE

I pulled the Lionel train set, which the Robinsons had given to me as a gift for that 1948 Hanukkah, out of the box my father had saved for me. I still have the most amazing memories from the celebration. My favorite was watching Jackie charm my bubbe into accepting the tree as a symbol of friendship and shared humanity. I also loved watching my father pray for peace, understanding, and friendship and then turn to Jackie and smile. I learned that whether you are Christian or Jewish, we both pray to God. Jackie asked for equality and justice. Was that different from asking for peace?

For the first time, I beat my cousins at the dreidel game. Rachel's delicious apple pie was a hit. It was a holiday I will never duplicate or forget. Two months later, I received a package with hundreds of thank-you letters written to me from children throughout Israel. I read every one of them. At school, I shared the personal war stories with my class. My entire school raised thousands of dollars for UNICEF.

After the New Year, the Robinsons moved to St. Albans, Queens. I took the move hard, but I remembered that solid friendships are forever. When I had my tonsils out, Jackie visited me in the hospital. For my sixteenth birthday, he sent a baseball signed by all the 1955 World Champion Dodgers— after years of just falling short, the Dodgers had finally won a World Series!

Dad and I would see Jackie before games at Ebbets Field and on his occasional visits to Tilden Avenue. But Jackie retired from Major League Baseball after the 1956 season. He was thirty-six. He and Rachel had built a beautiful home in Stamford, Connecticut, and lived there with their three children, Jackie, Sharon, and David. Dad drove us up to visit them a couple of times so Jackie Junior and I could fish and take the rowboat out to the middle of the lake. Jackie loved the six-acre property. He said it gave his family the privacy and space they needed. As my father predicted and Jackie promised, we remained friends for life.

Reaching deeper inside the box, my fingers found a photo of dad and me at a Brooklyn Dodgers game. I carefully placed that picture in a pile on the floor on top of the opening day ticket stubs from when I had first met Jackie and Roy all those years ago.

There were other photos of my father with his parents and some of us with Mom. I pulled out a small jewelry box and opened it to find Dad's gold signet ring. I slipped it onto the ring finger of my left hand before continuing to plow through the box, where I found a crushed and faded Brooklyn Dodgers cap. I shouted with joy when I pulled out the baseball autographed by the entire 1955 World Champion Dodgers team.

At the very bottom of the box, I retrieved the mitt Jackie had given me when I was eight. The leather was stiff. The size was still wrong, but it brought back such wonderful memories.

Lying next to the mitt, wrapped in layers of tissue paper, I found the angel from my one and only Christmas tree. A breath caught in my chest. It was so thoughtful that my dad had saved all my childhood treasures. I left them scattered about my room and went downstairs to find my mother. We sat quietly in the dimly lit living room until I was ready to talk.

"Think Jackie knows about Dad?"

"I thought you should be the one to tell him, Stephen."

I looked at my mother's face, tired from the emotional ride she had been on recently. "Thank you, Mom." I said. "I'll go give Jackie a call now."

The next day I met Jackie at his Lexington Avenue office. He'd switched uniforms from Dodgers blue to a sharp-looking tailored black suit. He was a businessman now, leading employees and making a difference in their lives as he'd done in mine.

"Your dad was proud of you, Steve," Jackie told me. "He said you're planning on going to medical school. Is that right?"

"That was the plan," I replied. "Not so sure now."

"Why's that?"

"How will we afford it?"

"Just do your part and keep both your ambition and your grades up. The money will be there," Jackie assured me.

"Do you miss it?" I asked impulsively.

"Baseball, you mean?"

"Yes."

"Not at all," Jackie replied. "I love being home nights with my family. I enjoy my work here and I'm raising money for the civil rights movement. My life is full and good. You can't look back, Steve. You've got to keep moving on and up. You'll become your best self if you stay focused, set goals, and don't let anyone stop you from making your dreams come true." Jackie paused and looked at me. "Hanukkah and Christmas are a day apart again this year," he said.

"How'd you know that?" I asked, surprised.

"I keep up," Jackie said with a chuckle. "The year Rachel and I celebrated Hanukkah with your family was so special. Your grandmother gave me such a hard time over that tree."

I laughed. "As I remember it, you handled Bubbe with ease. She talked about you for years after that."

"That's it, Steve. When you reach out to others, good always comes back to you. I have a saying: 'A life is not important except for the impact it has on other lives.' "

"That makes sense, Jackie. Guess that's why I want to be a doctor."

"You'll be a great doctor—and hurry up. I need help keeping my diabetes under control," Jackie said.

"Give me a few years," I promised.

"Steve, we'd love to have you and your mom over for Christmas. Jackie, Sharon, and David would be so excited! It would mean the world to Rachel,"

Jackie suggested. "I'll ask her to make the arrangements with your mother. What do you say?"

"You mean in Connecticut?"

"That's right. Would you like that, Steve?"

"More than you know," I said, feeling happy for the first time since losing Dad.

Standing and drawing me into a bear hug, Jackie thanked me for coming to see him. "I know that you're in pain, but I hope you feel some comfort in knowing how much your dad loved you. Be strong, son. We'll see you again soon."

"Yes, see you again soon," I told him. I turned and left. Jackie's strength and friendship meant more to me now than ever.

AFTERWORD

*T*he Hero Two Doors Down is based on a
true story. It takes place in the Flatbush
section of Brooklyn in 1948. Stephen Satlow
truly lived two doors down from my parents, Jack
and Rachel Robinson. In reality, Steve was Sarah and
Archie's middle child. To keep the focus on Steve's
relationship with Jackie, I left out his sisters, Paula
and Sena. Steve's best friend is based on his sis-
ter Sena.

Since this story happened before I was born, my strongest memories are of my mother, father, and Steve's mother, Sarah, each sharing their reflections on the Christmas tree story. This family lore marked the beginning of a lifelong friendship between the Satlows and the Robinsons.

Steve did become a doctor and he and I have remained friends. Occasionally we ride horses on his Ocala, Florida, ranch, but mostly we sit back and marvel at the strength of the bond between our mothers. Sarah and Rachel are both deep into their nineties now, with hearing aids, strong legs, and determined spirits. They've become our heroes.

During these troubling times of global, racial, cultural, and religious unrest, I decided that this classic story of friendship and unity needed to be shared with the next generation of readers. While I maintained the integrity of the true story, this is partly a work of fiction. For example, Steve was actually six years old in 1948. He is an amazing storyteller. While we spent quiet afternoons on his ranch, he shared the richness of his Jewish Brooklyn childhood. Gradually, Steve's voice was firmly implanted in my head.

Throughout my life, I've encountered many passionate men and women who grew up in Brooklyn during the Brooklyn Dodgers era. The genuine affection for the Brooklyn Dodgers was matched by a profound sense of loss when the team moved west. But few stories could compete with the one told by Steve Satlow. In 1948, he lived the dream of millions of young boys. He lived two doors down from his hero.

Stephen Satlow, age seven, reading in 1949. (Photo courtesy of Stephen Satlow)

Jackie Robinson, Rachel Robinson, and Jackie Robinson Jr. on the steps of their Tilden Avenue home. (© Nina Leen Life Picture Collection/Getty Images)

Rachel Robinson and Sarah Cymrot, Steve's mom, remain friends to this day. (Photo courtesy of the Robinson family)

Still friends today, Sharon and Steve ride horses at the Satlow ranch in Ocala, Florida. (Photo courtesy of Izzy Satlow)

ACKNOWLEDGMENTS

First and foremost I'd like to open this page with a thank-you to all young readers! You're awesome! I hope you loved reading *The Hero Two Doors Down*. Were you able to picture becoming friends with your hero? I wish that for all of you!

I'd like to thank my amazing parents, Jack and Rachel Robinson, for their love and guidance and for teaching me the importance of preserving and passing along a strong family legacy. I learned to love books from my mother. Life with "RR," as I'm fond of calling my mom, is one long, wondrous journey! Our shared love for reading is part of that adventure.

I've had an incredible twenty-year partnership with Scholastic Inc.! This includes the operation of the Breaking Barriers program, co-run by Scholastic and Major League Baseball, which focuses on students' abilities to overcome obstacles in their lives.

I've also been fortunate to author several books for Scholastic. Our newest one, *The Hero Two Doors Down*, would not have been possible without the vibrant storytelling of our young hero, Stephen Satlow. I wish to thank Steve and his entire family, including his mother, Sarah Cymrot, for years of friendship as well as their guidance and best wishes on this project.

I want to thank my editor, Matt Ringler, who helped bring clarity and insight to my writing and the project as a whole. Thank you, Matt, for making the process seamless and fun! There are many others at Scholastic whom I'd like to thank especially: Dick Robinson, Ellie Berger, Charisse Meloto, Bess Braswell, Whitney Steller, Caitlin Friedman, Lizette Serrano, Judy Newman and her Book Clubs team, and Alan Boyko and his Book Fairs group.

The relationship between writer and literary agent is critical to moving a project from manuscript to published book. My agent, Katherine Cowles, has played such an important role in my life. Kitty, thank you for your keen insight, friendship, and vision!

I've worked with two incredible MLB Commissioners: Bud Selig and Rob Manfred. I owe a great deal of my professional growth to their enduring support. Along the way, I've made many friends at MLB who have been especially supportive of my writing: Jacqueline Parkes, Thomas Brasuell, Kevin Moss, Steve Arocho, Anne Occi, Claudia Vosper, David Kaufman, and Nick Trotta. A special thank-you to the New York Mets and the Los Angeles

Dodgers along with their players—especially Curtis Granderson (Mets), Michael Cuddyer (Mets), and Jimmy Rollins (Dodgers)—for their amazing support and contributions to the Scholastic video!

A very special thank-you to Della Britton Baeza, Gregg Gonsalves, Len Coleman, Marty Edelman, and the entire staff and board of the Jackie Robinson Foundation for your incredible work, love, and support!

Many, many thanks to friends who read each version of the manuscript and gave me invaluable feedback: Nancy Lerner, Steven Ungerleider, Lyman Carter, and Steve's wife, Izzy. And, last but not least, a special thank-you to my brother, David, to my nieces and nephews, and to my grandchildren, Jessica and Lucas.

You are all my sheroes and heroes. I'm blessed to call each of you my friend. If only you all lived two doors down . . .

SHARON ROBINSON, daughter of baseball legend Jackie Robinson, is the author of several works of fiction and nonfiction. She has also written several widely praised nonfiction books about her father, including *Jackie's Nine: Jackie Robinson's Values to Live By* and *Promises to Keep: How Jackie Robinson Changed America.*